"Say it... Three words.

"All right! I—"

Phil watched her carefully, one hand outstretched but not reaching for her. "It's not so hard, is it? Now once more. Finish it. I—"

Victoria drew in a deep, shuddering breath. She did, she really did love this man. "I—"

"Love—" Phil prompted.

The word hung in her throat. "I—"

"Come on, baby, just two more words. That's all."

"I—" With a moan she flung herself against Phil's chest. "I love you." Saying it once freed her voice. "I love you, Phil. I love you." *I love you*. Simple words. Words people said every day.

ABOUT THE AUTHOR

Modean Moon can't remember a time that
she didn't want to write; she started a
writing club when she was eight and wrote
her first novel at fourteen. She is now a
petroleum landman, writing in her spare
time. Modean lives in a restored Victorian
farmhouse overlooking the town of Poteau,
Oklahoma.

Books by Modean Moon

HARLEQUIN AMERICAN ROMANCE
77–DARE TO DREAM
113–HIDING PLACES
146–AN UNCOMMON HERO

Don't miss any of our special offers. Write to us at the
following address for information on our newest releases.

Harlequin Reader Service
901 Fuhrmann Blvd., P.O. Box 1397, Buffalo, NY 14240
Canadian address: P.O. Box 603,
Fort Erie, Ont. L2A 5X3

Simple
Words
Modean Moon

Harlequin Books

TORONTO • NEW YORK • LONDON
AMSTERDAM • PARIS • SYDNEY • HAMBURG
STOCKHOLM • ATHENS • TOKYO • MILAN

Published November 1988

First printing September 1988

ISBN 0-373-16271-5

Chapter One

Perverse. That was the only word Victoria Tankersley could think of to describe that entire Friday.

Perverse Oklahoma weather. How many Christmases had she prayed for snow only to find herself surrounded by sunshine and wearing no more than a light sweater? Now, barely into November, the wind was spitting out of the north, penetrating her winter work coat and chilling her in spite of the garment's fleece lining. She'd be lucky if the area didn't get a full-fledged storm, complete with icy roads and frozen mornings for winter feeding.

Perverse. In swift succession she applied the word to her father, for choosing the rankest replacement cow he could possibly find to add to their herd, to Will Hastings, the son of the owner of the sale barn, who was supposed to be helping her load that cow into the trailer, but was instead having a high old time sitting on the fence rail and watching her struggle with the cow, a massive yellow, wild-eyed, high-horned beast of indeterminate and indiscriminate cross-breeding.

"Horns, for God's sake," she muttered under her breath. "Why on earth did he have to pick another one with horns?" But she knew. After twenty years in

the hills of southeastern Oklahoma, her father still
ranched as he had in his youth, as his father had before him, on the high desert of New Mexico. And, this
was probably the most important reason, the cow had
come cheap. Making do with the inexpensive in order
to survive had become very important almost over-
night. And circumstances had remained that way for
so many years that remembering how things had been
before took on an aura of unreality.

"You say something, Vic?" Will Hastings called
out.

Victoria swirled around to glare at the teenager and
felt more of her hair crawl out of its pins and slither
inside her hat.

"Come on, Vic," Will taunted. "Show us what a
good cowboy you are."

Victoria was a good cowhand. After being raised on
a ranch and having ten years of steady experience in a
saddle, she couldn't help but be one. But her five feet
five inches and one hundred and ten pounds were no
match for the twelve hundred pounds of bovine beauty
that was rapidly destroying what was left of a generally
lousy day.

Well, she couldn't wrestle the cow, and there was no
way she was going to walk into the trailer and try to
lead it in, no way she was going to risk trapping herself between those horns and the trailer rails, but by
God, she could at least outthink the animal.

For a moment she studied the cow, the trailer and
the problem, then, taking a firmer grip on the rope,
she glared at the cow. "Come on, you long-legged,
bony, cantankerous bag of walking dog food, you *are*
getting in that trailer, and we *are* going home."

PHIL WILCOX STEPPED out of the sale barn to be greeted by a chill blast of air. He tugged his jacket closed and hoped that this particular cold front was some sort of meteorological problem and not the beginning of winter. The hay crop hadn't been all that good, and a harsh winter could mean disaster for the small ranchers.

From the number of cattle run through the sale today, he suspected that the ranchers were taking no chances, cutting their losses while they could, culling their herds and selling while the market price was still decent.

Phil hadn't come to the sale to buy or to sell livestock. He had an appointment with Sam Hastings, the sale barn owner, but from the looks of things, it would be a while before Sam had finished collecting and distributing the day's proceeds. Phil was early, but he didn't really mind. He glanced around at the organized confusion, the large tractor-trailer rigs of the feedlots, the packing plants and the order buyers and the steel-railed pens full of bawling, milling cattle. There was something about the sights, sounds, even the smells of a cattle sale that made him feel at home.

And since Sam's teenage son, Will, was the purpose of the appointment, Phil decided that he could put the extra time to good use. Will wouldn't like it, but then he didn't like much of anything these days, including the fact that his father was making him work the sale.

Phil found Will a few minutes later, not working as he was supposed to be, but sitting on a fence rail with a couple of his friends, jeering at another boy attempting to load a yellow, horned cow into a battered trailer. He couldn't tell much about the boy other than his diminutive stature because of the bulky coat and pulled-down black cowboy hat, but he knew it had to be a kid. Will was only a bully with someone younger and smaller than he. But it wasn't a boy, Phil noted as the wind caught and twisted the coat revealing a girl. And she was much too small to be doing what she was trying to do.

Phil studied the scene a moment and then stepped forward. He had to give the kid credit. At least she hadn't trapped herself in the trailer with the cow. Pulling the rope through the trailer and bringing it outside had been a good idea, but the rope wasn't long enough for her to work her way back to the cow, and Phil knew that the animal wasn't going to move without more encouragement than she was getting. And why wasn't the girl's father here to help her?

Without giving his actions a second thought, Phil walked to the side of the cow. "You pull," he yelled at the girl. "I'll get her started."

VICTORIA RECOGNIZED the voice, but she stole a quick look over her shoulder at the redheaded and bearded man standing behind the trailer. *Oh, God,* she thought, *Phil Wilcox.* She ought to tell him she didn't need his help, that the only thing she wanted was for him to get away from her and anything she or her father still owned. But being the realist she had become, she knew she couldn't turn down his offer. She nodded her head in agreement, feeling still more hair come loose, and took a firm hold on the rope.

Phil swatted the cow's flank with a solid blow at the same time he gave a yell, and the cow lunged forward, up the ramp and into the trailer with the speed, if not the grace, of a thoroughbred horse. Quickly,

Victoria secured the rope. Slowly, she turned to face Phil. Give the devil his due, she urged herself. The man helped you. The least you can do is say thanks.

The grudging thanks died unspoken in her throat. Phil slammed the trailer gate shut and glanced over at her, an impersonal smile on his face. "There you go, young lady. Next time, ask for help, or you'll get yourself hurt."

Victoria didn't know what incensed her the most; that he thought she was a callow, inexperienced kid or that in spite of all they had been through, he didn't even know who she was. She snatched her hat from her head, feeling pins and black hair tumbling over her shoulders. Of course, he had never seen her as a woman; he hadn't seen her at all for years. The last time they saw each other she had been an adversary, a victim in a thwarted foreclosure that he was handling for the bank. Before the problems with the ranch she had been just another teenage girl, of no consequence to a rising young attorney. But not even to remember her? She choked back a bitter laugh at the sight of Phil Wilcox's stunned expression when he recognized her.

"Victoria," he said with a swift expulsion of breath. "I—when did you get back? I'm—"

So he did remember her after all. *I've been back for nine years,* she thought. *You saw to that.* But she wouldn't tell him that. And at this moment, listening to a stammered, insincere apology offended her more than his original mistake. She owed him a thank you and no more. Eyes flashing, she glared at him. "Thanks. I'll make a note of your advice," she said before she turned on her boot heel and stalked off.

Perverse, she thought as she went in search of her father, who was probably still drinking coffee with his cronies near the cashier's office. The whole damned day had been perverse. Don't take it out on Pop, she warned herself. She knew it had to be every bit as hard on him as it was on her, probably tougher, not being able to work the cattle anymore, not even being able to ride a horse.

She felt the sting of moisture in her eyes. "Damned wind," she muttered as she reached the door to the office and yanked it open.

TWO HOURS OF TALKING with Sam and Will Hastings, trying to explain to the boy why he couldn't hotwire his father's truck and drive anywhere he wanted, why he couldn't insult any police officer just because his uncle was deputy sheriff, and what was going to happen to him if he continued to do so, hadn't done one thing to diminish Phil's memory of Victoria's expression when she whirled away from him.

What was she doing here? It must have been five or six years—no, he remembered ruefully, wondering where the time had gone, it had been closer to nine years—since he had last seen her. But not to recognize her? It had to have been that shapeless coat and the pulled-down hat and the fact that he never expected to see Victoria Tankersley in a cattle lot.

There had never been any question of not recognizing Victoria when she had been a fresh-faced teenager going through a serious tomboy stage. And certainly not the last time he saw her at the foreclosure. She must have been twenty, maybe a little older. He'd been drawn to her then, but an impossible situation stood between them—a nasty lawsuit.

When he thought about her afterward—and he admitted to himself that he had—he assumed she had gone back to that fancy Eastern university and married the man who had put that enormous square-cut diamond on her finger.

Phil pushed his disturbing thoughts of Victoria Tankersley to the back of his mind when he pulled into his driveway and parked. He was later than he had planned to be, but Angela was still home. He knew that, the moment he opened the front door to his comfortable, sprawling farm-styled home a few miles outside the city limits of Hillsboro and heard the beat of rock music coming from the direction of her bedroom.

"Angela!" he called out, tossing his hat at the hall tree. "I'm home."

Abruptly the noise level dropped. Phil smiled. At least some of the younger generation had respect for rules and consideration for others. He wandered through the house, into the kitchen, where dinner waited on the stove. *Some* consideration for others, he amended. He was hungry, steak and potatoes hungry, and his daughter had decided to try out another new recipe. He grimaced and replaced the lid on the pot. She was trying, he reminded himself. And it did smell good. And maybe, this time, she had made enough.

He heard the rustle of cloth behind him and turned toward her. "How was your trip to the orthodontist...?" His voice deserted him. For a moment, all he could do was stare at his daughter. Angela was six feet tall, only four inches shorter than he, and slender; those were undeniable facts. Another undeniable fact was that the young woman facing him bore only a passing resemblance to the coltish child he'd breakfasted with that morning. Gone were the blue jeans and sweatshirt. Gone was the long braid he had affectionately tugged as she started out the door to school. She wore something long and floating, probably her own creation, a mishmash of colors that should have clashed with the mane of red hair falling free almost to her waist, and makeup, subtly and skillfully applied to make her look much older than her not quite eighteen.

She stood completely still while he stared at her, then smiled, opening her lips wide to expose beautifully straight white teeth. "They're gone," she said. She laughed and spun around, becoming once again his daughter. "Oh, Dad, it feels so good to get rid of those braces."

She ran across the room and hugged him exuberantly. "I hated them, you know, and sometimes I got so mad at you for making me wear them." She laughed again, opened her mouth and clicked her teeth together. "But it was worth it. It was all worth it. Thanks, Dad."

At dinner that night, Angela reverted to her adult pose, presiding over an elegantly set table, a delicious meal, and giving him more than a glimpse of the beautiful woman she was fast becoming.

Whatever happened, he wondered, to the squalling bundle of red hair and pink flesh he had held such a short time ago, to the skinny little pigtailed girl who had run to him with her scraped knees and runny nose, to the shy teenager who had hesitantly confessed to him that at long last she had a boyfriend.

"I'm going to miss those braces," he thought aloud.

Angela looked up at him and frowned. "There's something else you're going to miss," she said hesitantly.

"What, Pinkie?" For the first time, he felt the need to use her ridiculous nickname, to remind him that she was after all, still his little girl.

"You never call me that."

He just shook his head.

"Never mind," she said, sighing.

"What am I going to miss?" he prompted.

She looked at him steadily, pursing her lips in thought. "Me," she said. "I mean, I'm going away to college next year, and while it will be all right for me—I'll be making new friends, you know—you're going to be left here all alone, and I'll worry about you, Dad, so I've been giving some serious thought about what to do, and I've come up with an answer to the problem."

"Oh?" Phil asked, leaning back in his chair as he took a sip of coffee. "And just what answer have you come up with?"

"Simple," Angela told him. "You're going to get married again."

Phil choked, he coughed and he hurriedly set the coffee cup on the table before he splashed any more of the liquid on himself.

"It's the only answer," Angela told him calmly. "And I'm surprised I didn't think of it sooner."

"You . . . have someone picked out?" Phil asked.

"No. Not yet. There really isn't anyone in Hillsboro, you know. And I've pretty well eliminated the available women in the surrounding area."

"There's always Hazel," he suggested, wanting to puncture her serious mood.

"Hazel?" she asked. "At the Korner Kaff? Da-ad!"

"What's wrong with Hazel?" he asked, fighting a smile.

"Nothing. She's a lovely person. She just weighs as much as you do." She grinned at him. "I thought maybe we could advertise."

"Angela Wilcox, if you have dared to put an ad in any publication—"

"No." She held her hand out. "No, I haven't. Not yet. I wanted to discuss it with you first."

Phil expelled a deep breath and forced himself to relax in his chair. "I can see it now," he said, " 'Big strapping redheaded man, in his dotage, wishes companion for his lonely golden years.' "

"Come on, Dad, be serious. Besides, you're not in your dotage. You're younger than Tom Selleck. And you're as good-looking as he is. I mean, you don't look like him, except you're both . . . big, but—"

"I get the picture, Angela," he told her, knowing that if he didn't she would probably stammer around all night.

"And anyway," she continued. "You don't really have to tell them a lot. You can ask for what you want."

Once again he picked up his coffee cup. It seemed safe. Surely nothing else she said would shock him into spilling any more. "And what *do* I want?"

"Well," she said, pushing her plate aside and resting her elbows on the table, "the way I see it—you're bright and educated, so you need a woman who is the same, too. And sometimes, when you're not being Clarence Darrow or Lord of the Manor, you can be a real teddy bear, so you need a woman to bring out that part of you, someone who is soft and warm and feminine."

Phil was surprised at his daughter's perception, but it wasn't a bad picture she was painting.

"And tall," he added.

Angela nodded her head. "Oh, definitely. I can't see you with a short woman. You'd have a terminal crick in your neck." Angela darted a look at him, colored slightly and ducked her head. "Or she would."

Phil fumbled his coffee cup and once again set it on the table. There were other requirements he could think of in a woman, but not many that he would share with his seventeen-year-old daughter. "While we're building this paragon," he said, when he felt sure enough that his voice would work, "we might as well make her a blonde."

"Super." Angela pushed back from the table. "Let me get a notebook."

"Angela." His softly growled use of her name stopped her. "No ad."

Her face fell, and she slumped back in her chair. "I'm just trying to do what's best for you," she said. "Isn't that what you're always telling me you're doing?"

He looked at her and sighed. "I know, honey, and I appreciate your good intentions. But when the time comes for me to get married again, I'll know it. And when I meet the right woman, I'll know that, too."

Later, after Angela had left to spend the night with a girlfriend in town, Phil lay in bed, alone in the empty house, thinking back on the last of a long line of surprising conversations he had had with his daughter over the years. She was right; he needed someone. His whole adult life had been devoted to raising his daughter, finishing law school, building his practice, overseeing his ranch and being there when any member of his extended family needed him. For years he hadn't had time to be lonely; now he did. Now he was.

He called up the image of the woman he and Angela had invented. Tall, blonde, bright and educated. Feminine. He knew that with the reality of morning he would reject Angela's misguided plan, but for the moment he let himself succumb to the fantasy. Someone who was comfortable with being a woman. And sensual. That was one attribute he hadn't seen fit to mention to his daughter. Seductive. As he drifted toward sleep, he found the image wavering. He tried to hold on to it, but he couldn't. The last thing his mind saw that night was black hair tumbling around the elfin face and over the shoulders of Victoria Tankersley and her black eyes glittering at him with a chill that no Oklahoma winter had ever produced.

VICTORIA TOSSED another log on the fireplace and prodded the fire to life before curling up in the corner of the sofa with a book. It was late; she didn't really want to know just how late it was. The chores were done, supper finished and the dishes cleaned away, Pop in bed, herself bathed and shampooed. Tomorrow morning she would have to get up early to feed the cattle. Tomorrow morning she would have to do something about that damned yellow cow, now penned in a lot near the barn. She knew she ought to be working on the paper that was due in her first class Monday night, but for these few minutes she had decided her time was her own.

She wore a long white flannel nightgown. All things being equal, she probably would have bought it anyway because it was warm, but the touch of lace and the detailing gave it a Victorian air. Granted, the effect was slightly spoiled by the long white socks she wore to keep her feet warm, but some things she wasn't willing to give up, not even for fantasy.

She glanced around the room. The furniture had belonged to her mother, a soft, Southern lady with a strong backbone and a strength of will to match; a woman who had married her cowboy in spite of her family's opposition, and in spite of his. True, the classic English lines were somewhat incongruous in the tiny white frame house, and the upholstery had long since passed the "getting shabby" stage, but all in all it was a comfortable room, a pleasant room. Even Josh and Jimbo, the two half-Shepherd, half-Collie cow dogs agreed with her on that as they dozed by the fireplace.

The book, another treasure from the used book store near the college campus, old but not valuable, tempted her. It was an early twentieth-century reprint of a still earlier best seller. Her major advisor at Vassar would be appalled. But then, she didn't have to worry about him anymore. There would be no literature degree from Vassar, no master's degree, no Ph.D., no faculty position at an Eastern university, no happily ever after with Brad.

Damn you, Phil Wilcox, she thought bitterly. She hadn't counted her losses in years. If this was what seeing him did to her, she was grateful this was a large county. She wasn't being entirely fair to him, she knew that. He had only been the attorney for the bank. But he hadn't needed to do such a *good* job. And it was hard to focus anger on a bank, especially since that bank had gone out of business two years later. And especially since she had once thought the sun rose and set on Phil Wilcox.

She picked up the book and opened it defiantly. She wasn't going to think about Phil Wilcox, she didn't have to worry about her major adviser anymore, and this time was hers to do with what she saw fit, and she saw fit to read nineteenth-century romance.

Why? she wondered as she stared at the frontispiece. Why romance of the past? Maybe it was because of stories her mother had told her about growing up. Maybe it was half-remembered stories of her grandmother. Whatever the reason, Victoria realized she was viewing life through the rose-colored glasses of fiction, but that didn't really matter to her. Fiction was fantasy on paper; fantasy stemmed from real people, from their dreams, from their desires. And in the fantasy of nineteenth-century fiction, man might scoff at woman, he might impede her progress, but he didn't laugh at her, and he didn't expect her to be able to hold up the world single-handedly. Woman didn't have to deny that man was physically stronger than she was; she could admit to being tired, to being lonely, to being less than perfect. Good Lord, when the going got too tough, she could even faint.

Feeling sorry for yourself, Victoria? She could almost hear her mother's soft, melodic voice. *I suppose it's natural, but life's too short to spend on self-pity, so give yourself a good two minutes to wallow in it and then get on with the business of living.* Victoria smiled at the path her thoughts had taken. There was one good thing about the schedule she was constantly shuffling; she didn't have two minutes to waste. Maybe one. And she had already used that.

"Vickie?"

Victoria closed her book and sat up in alarm. "Yes, Pop?"

Her father appeared at the end of the hall. Her heart broke to look at him, a once tall, once proud man now stopped over his cane. "I heard something down at the barn."

Victoria glanced at the two dogs, still sleeping peacefully. "Josh and Jimbo didn't," she said without thinking.

Her father snorted in disgust. "Worthless hounds. Give them a full belly and a warm bed, and they'd sleep through a tornado. I think I'll just go have a look."

Victoria wouldn't argue with him about the dogs but she would about the rest of his statement. There was probably nothing wrong at the barn, but if there was, her father didn't need to be wandering into it. He'd had one stroke and a heart attack already. No stress, the doctor had told them. For a man who had been active most of his life, who had ruled his family and everything else in his domain with an iron hand, obeying that rule had to be a miserable way to live out the rest of his days. But obey it, he would, if Victoria had anything to do about it. Otherwise there wouldn't be any days for him to live out.

"I'll go," she said, unwinding from the couch. "It's probably just that replacement cow kicking up a fuss."

Her father met her gaze in a silent contest of wills before he nodded in quiet acquiescence. "Take the dogs."

"I will." She walked to the door and pulled her boots on over her white socks. "Josh! Jimbo! Wake up, you lazy critters." She heard the wind moaning outside. Ice before morning, she thought wearily. Then she tugged on her coat over her nightgown and plunked her hat down on her wet head. There was probably nothing there, but on the almost negligible chance that some animal had wandered down from the wooded hills behind their place, she lifted a shotgun from the rack and stepped outside.

For an instant in her mind she saw Phil Wilcox's face, looking at her, seeing how different her life was now from how she had once haughtily told him it would be.

Perverse, she thought, as she bent into the wind and headed toward the silent barn. The whole lousy day had been perverse.

Chapter Two

She could do it. Victoria stood defiantly staring at the yellow cow standing just as defiantly in the center pen of their motley assortment of wooden and metal corrals. Of course she could do it. She *had* to do it.

The noise the night before had been made by the cow, just as she thought. Unfortunately, it had been made by the cow connecting with one of the wooden corral rails, splintering the rail and leaving a long ragged gash along the animal's right hind leg. And just as unfortunately, Pop's sharp eyes had spotted it first thing that morning when they'd gone out to feed.

"We'll take care of that when I get back from town," he told her. "Don't let her out with the herd until then."

As if she would have. Victoria had more sense than to do that. And she had more sense than to wait until he returned from his doctor's appointment to treat the wound. If she waited, she'd not only have the cow to contend with, she'd have Pop in the pen with her, trying to do the work himself or telling her in step-by-step detail how to do something she knew as well as he how to do.

At least it wasn't icy. The early-morning frost had already burned off. And with the temperature slightly warmer than the day before, she wasn't hampered by her heavy work coat. She was chilled in the padded vest over her jeans and flannel shirt, but not unbearably so.

She pursed her lips, settled her hat firmly on her head and glared at the cow. "Okay, lady," she said softly. "It's me against you. And don't think for a moment that I'm not going to win."

As PHIL TURNED off the country road and up the long, winding drive to the Tankersley ranch, he suspected that he was about to make a fool of himself. He wasn't completely sure of his motives for coming. He had a vague idea of apologizing to Victoria for his mistake of the day before. He had a vague idea that he might be chased off the property with a loaded shotgun. He even had a vague idea that the Tankersleys might be within their rights to do so. All of those thoughts settled uneasily around him in the cab of his pickup truck.

All he knew for sure was that Victoria Tankersley had disturbed his sleep the night before. He had to see her again, to prove to himself that there was as little comparison between her and the woman of his dreams as there was between her and the girl he had mistaken her for. And he was disturbed that he hadn't known before now she was home, wrestling with cows and looking as though she had a lot of practice at it, and not back East, where she had once sworn to him she belonged.

The house looked empty, Phil thought, as he stopped his truck in a parking area near the kitchen door. Not even a dog came out to challenge him, which was unusual in this rural area. Of course, they could be working. Ranch chores didn't stop on weekends.

He stepped from his truck, glancing once more at the house. It needed a coat of paint, he noted absently before scanning the barn and corrals. Everything needed a coat of paint. He heard a dog bark from the direction of the corrals and sharpened his gaze. And Victoria Tankersley needed her head examined. There was no mistaking her today, in a pen with her two dogs and the same yellow cow she had been having so much trouble with the day before. Was she trying to get herself killed? On that thought, Phil took off running toward the corral.

"GOOD GOING," Victoria told Josh and Jimbo, as, barking and nipping at her heels, they urged the cow through still another gate. Just one more, and she would have the animal where she wanted her.

"What in the *hell* do you think you're doing?"

Startled, Victoria looked up to see angry gray eyes glaring at her as Phil Wilcox hooked a boot on the bottom rail of the corral and started to lift himself over. Her heart gave a strange lurch, which she immediately attributed to anger. Without any particular trouble on her part, she had managed not to see him for almost nine years. Now, seeing him twice in two days was twice too often.

She slammed the gate, blocking the cow's escape, and directed her glare toward Phil. "I don't *think* I'm doing anything, Mr. Wilcox. I'm *doing* it."

He vaulted over the top rail lightly, in spite of his size, and stood towering over her, angry far beyond any reason Victoria could see. "By yourself?" he asked. His voice boomed through the quiet morning, silencing the remaining bird calls and causing the cow to snort and sidle farther away.

Just who did he think had been carrying the load of this place since the bank had reneged on its promises? Her voice rising to match her rising anger, she tilted her head and yelled back at him, "Do you *see* anybody else?"

Something in her anger must have touched him. She saw his lips twitch within the fullness of his well-trimmed beard and mustache and then part in a smile. "Where's your father?"

Being the object of his humor was more objectionable to her than his thinking she was an incompetent. Victoria took a step back from him and, resting one fist on her canted hip, took a deep breath. "He's in town."

"And you just couldn't wait until he returned."

Victoria blew out her breath. "Mr. Wilcox," she said evenly. "My father is at the doctor's office, where he has a regular, standing appointment. That cow has a foot-long gash in her right leg that has to be treated before I can let her out into the pasture. If I waited for Pop's return, if I let him do what I'm getting ready to do, in all probability I'd have to take him back to the doctor's office, if not the emergency room."

Phil's smile faded. "I didn't know," he said softly.

And whose fault is that? Victoria wondered. *After all, we do live in the same county.*

"You don't have a hired hand?" he asked.

Victoria shook her head.

"A neighbor who could help?"

Good Lord, *now* he was going to pity her, and she didn't want his pity any more than she wanted anything else from the hulk of a man looming over her. He was so damned sure of himself, so confident of his abilities. He probably didn't even let the weather bother him; he probably generated enough body heat so that he didn't even feel the chill through the long-sleeved shirt bonded to his broad shoulders and massive chest.

"Mr. Wilcox," she said evenly, "you obviously have a reason for being here, or you wouldn't be here, so would you please state that reason and go on about your business, so that I can put that cow where she belongs and go on about mine."

Phil eased his hat to the back of his head and turned to look at the cow. "She belongs in a freezer," he said flatly.

His words echoed Victoria's sentiments, but she couldn't tell him that. "We don't need that much hamburger, and that's all she's good for except for raising calves. We do need the calves."

"Okay," he said companionably. "Then let's get to work."

"Work?" Victoria asked weakly. "Us?"

"Look," Phil told her, "you don't have a hired hand, you don't have a neighbor who can help right now. I'm here. You hadn't planned on getting her in the squeeze chute by yourself, had you?"

He was here. He did know cattle. And he was strong. He could help. If she would just bend her pride a little and let him. "No," she admitted, remembering how she had worried about just that problem. "I was going to trap her in the alley."

He glanced down at her and sighed. "Right," he said. "We don't have to worry about that now, do we?"

She looked up at him and hated herself when she heard her answering sigh. "No. We don't."

STUBBORN! For her size, Victoria Tankersley had to be the stubbornest, most unyielding female Phil had met in his entire life. He had a strong suspicion she had wanted to tell him to take a flying leap rather than accept his offer of help, but she had accepted. And then she had tackled the job with a competence that amazed him. He'd helped, but it had been clear to him from the beginning that she was in charge.

Victoria had insisted on operating the levers for the metal squeeze chute and head gate, trapping the cow once Phil had harassed it through the alley and into them. Victoria had let him snub the cow's head and right leg, but then she had taken over the treatment, examining and cleaning the wound and spraying it with antiseptic, inadvertently giving Phil a view of her trim backside as she knelt to retrieve supplies from the medical kit and then swiveled back toward the cow.

Definitely not a young girl, he thought again as he had so many times since the day before. But feminine? He winced when he heard her sharp curse at the cow, which in spite of the snubbing ropes and metal bars holding her had still managed to rear up in the chute.

"Are you all right?" he asked quickly.

"I'm fine," Victoria muttered, rising to her feet and wiping her hands on her thighs, drawing his attention to another trim part of her anatomy. Phil swallowed once and forced his eyes upward and his errant thoughts away from the long, shapely thighs of the Victoria in his troubled dreams.

"And she will be, too, in a day or so," Victoria said, marching around to the controls on the other side of the chute. "Let's turn her loose."

Phil glanced at the corral walls. In this pen they were a mixture of fixed wooden fences and movable metal gates, which could be opened or closed to form passageways or smaller pens. The ones to the front of the headgate were designed so that they created an alley out to a larger pen or blocked any medicated cattle in the pen with the chute. He wasn't in any danger—a half-closed gate protected him, but the way the other gates were arranged, the now audibly and visibly irate cow would have to stay in the pen with Victoria.

"You want to change those gates?"

"No," Victoria called back to him over the noise the cow was making. "I want her in this pen. She'll swing wide when she comes out. They always do."

They might always, but this cow bothered Phil. He looked over the back of it to Victoria, who suddenly looked small and vulnerable as she grasped the metal levers that would free the cow. "At least let me come over and do that," he suggested.

"Wilcox." Her tone brooked no argument.

"Right," he muttered and released the snub ropes.

He heard the clang of metal and the bawling of the cow as she stumbled and plunged her way out of confinement and then swung wide, as Victoria had said she would, snorting her displeasure. He met Victoria's steady gaze through the bars of the chute and felt irrationally pleased with her skill and her knowledge. "Good job," he said softly.

Her expression softened in a reluctant smile. "You, too," she said.

Their gazes locked for a moment, holding them both still. Phil recognized the current that ran between them—physical attraction—and at that moment he stopped lying to himself about why he had come to see her. In his dreams he had recognized the pull, even if it had taken his conscious mind hours longer to catch up.

She turned away first, slowly, and started walking toward the corral fence. He watched her for a moment, recognizing the futility of any desire he felt for her, then knelt to pick up the box of veterinary supplies. At first the dogs' barks were mere background noises for his turbulent thoughts. Then they penetrated those thoughts, and Phil looked up, puzzled.

The yellow cow had swung wide, all right, and had run to the opposite end of the pen. Now, still angry, it had turned, seeking and finding an outlet for its fury.

Dropping the box, Phil scrambled to his feet, drawing air into his lungs to yell a warning as he began running, knowing with a certainty that chilled the blood in his veins that he was going to be too late.

"VICTORIA! RUN!" She heard Phil's roared warning and the dogs at the same time. Pausing, she looked over her shoulder and froze at the sight of the yellow cow, horns lowered, bearing down her. She stood immobile for only a second, but that was a second she knew she couldn't spare, before sprinting for the fence. She hooked her foot on the bottom rail, her hands on the top, and began scrambling. Then, knowing she could never outclimb the raging cow, she kicked up from the fence, attempting to vault over it.

Her feet went up, but her body dropped lower. She heard angry hoofbeats over the pounding of the blood in her veins, felt a stunning blow to her midsection, heard the splintering of the wooden fence, and then Phil was there, swearing at the cow, beating it away from her, calling out to her.

The pressure was gone. She let her feet slide to the ground, but she couldn't release her death grip on the top fence rail. *God!* she thought, she could have been killed. In a matter of seconds, with no warning, she could have died.

She felt Phil's hands on her own, gentle in spite of their size, releasing her grip on the fence and then turning her to face him.

"How badly are you hurt?" he asked hoarsely.

"Hurt?" she heard the croak impersonating as her voice and tried again. "I'm not hurt," she said, wanting nothing more than to let herself sink against the security of his very warm, very close, very tempting body. *Stop that!* she warned herself. Thinking about his body was what had gotten her into this mess to start with. If that moment of eye contact hadn't completely addled her senses, if she hadn't let herself get lost in an impossible fantasy of herself and the man who now gripped her shoulders as though he was the only thing holding her up, she would have heard the dogs before she did, she would have heard the cow.

She tossed back her head and tried to ignore the lines of strain she saw etched in Phil's face, the concern she saw in his narrowed gray eyes. "It takes more than a little thing like that to hurt me," she said as she watched his face and eyes wavering before her. "It takes—" She lost her voice and started again. "It takes...."

VICTORIA WEIGHED practically nothing, and she was so still. She was deathly pale, her head thrown back, exposing a fragile, vulnerable throat, and some of her hair had come loose from its knot, spilling over his arm. He shouldn't have moved her. Phil knew that. But after catching her in his arms when she fell, he couldn't lay her on the muddy ground of the corral, or on the cold stubble of pasture-grass lawn. He eased open the kitchen door, kicked it shut behind them and hurried through the silent house.

At least there was no blood; that had been his first fear, that at least one of those horns had pierced her. Her bedroom was the first on the left down the short hall. It was obviously her bedroom, but Phil's mind only intuitively recognized that as he carried Victoria to the bed and laid her carefully on it.

She'd kill him if he got the pristine blue bedspread muddy; his mind recognized that intuitively, too. Knowing he was avoiding the worst of the issue, he tugged off one of her boots, then the other. Tiny feet, his mind registered as he held one cradled in his huge palm, even swathed in thick, wool socks. Then, easing onto the bed beside her, he fumbled with the buttons of her shirt.

He had never felt so clumsy, or so much an intruder. She wasn't going to like this, but he had no choice, he told himself as he finally freed the bottom buttons and spread her shirt open. He drew in a sharp breath and hesitated, hands poised over her. Small, yes. His hands could easily span her waist. Soft skin that could never have been exposed to the harsh rays of the sun caressed her ribs, dipped to the gentle hollow of her navel, and then flared to slender hips hidden beneath her low-cut jeans. That skin was now reddening, as early signs of discoloration spread their angry paths across her. Along her ribs, on the left side, ran a long, red abrasion.

Abrasion, Phil noted with a deep sigh. The horns that caught her as she twisted to vault the fence hadn't even punctured the skin.

With hands that were now trembling, Phil touched the red welt. He felt Victoria stir, then become rigidly still for a moment before she grabbed for his hands.

"Lie still," he said unsteadily.

"No!" Catching one of his hands in both of hers, she twisted violently beneath him. "Stop it, Phil!"

He heard the note of panic in her voice and raised his head to look at her face. He saw anger in her dark eyes, confusion, and a hint of fear.

"Victoria," he said, suddenly, intensely aware of her slight weight beneath him, of her breasts still covered by the soft flannel shirt, rising and falling in agitation. "I don't know how bad you're hurt," he told her as gently as he could.

"I'm fine—"

"Your shirt is torn." He met the angry glare of her eyes and held it. "You've got what could have been a nasty gash along your ribs, and God knows what else. Please!" he said a little desperately. "Please be still."

She looked away first, turning her head from him and closing her eyes, and he felt the fight go out of her as she slumped against the bed.

Once again he felt clumsy and inadequate. "Victoria?"

"Yes?"

"I'm going to touch you now," he told her, not wanting a replay of her earlier panic. "You understand that I have to, don't you?"

"Yes," she said tightly. "I understand."

She might understand but he didn't. The woman was injured, and what should have been an impersonal examination to find out just how badly she was injured was rapidly turning into a test of his self-control. He pressed his hands to her hip and felt her involuntarily flinch away from his touch.

"Does that hurt?" he asked.

"No."

"That?"

"No."

He worked his hands upward, forcing his touch to remain impersonal, until he reached her ribs.

"Breathe," he demanded unevenly. "Again." He felt the even rise and fall of her breath beneath his gently probing hands. "Any sharp pain?"

"No."

He let his hands lie still on her and dropped his head, sighing deeply. "You need X rays to be sure, but I think you're going to get off with just some serious bruising. I'll take you to the hospital now."

"No." He felt her let out her own deeply held breath. "It was a near miss, that's all. There's no need for a hospital bill just to confirm that."

She was probably right, but he wanted to argue with her. He wanted to scoop her up in his arms and carry her to the hospital no matter how much she protested. He wanted someone else, a doctor trained in these things, to tell him she was right. But he didn't do that either.

He lowered his head until it rested just above the softness of her breasts. "I was so afraid," he admitted.

"Me, too," she said in a little voice.

He felt movement beside him, Victoria raising her hand—would she touch him?—and then heard the soft rustle as she lowered it back to the bed.

"I thought you were dead," he said, knowing he should stop but not able to. "I saw those horns go around you, and all I could think of was what they could do to you."

"I hate horns," she told him, her voice breaking in the first sign of weakness she had ever given him.

He lifted his head. Closing her shirt over her, he smiled. "They probably saved your life. They hit the fence. That's what kept you from taking the full force of her charge."

"Silver linings, Wilcox?" she asked, giving him a shaky smile. "As in 'each cloud has one'?"

"Yeah," he said, pulling away from her. He had to do that or lean closer. "Look, what time will your dad be home?"

Victoria glanced at the clock near her bed. "Soon," she said. "Within the hour."

He shouldn't leave her alone, but he knew he needed some space away from her. "You're sure you're all right?" She wasn't; he knew that too. She was bruised and shaken and confused by his abrupt mood change.

"Sure," she said. "It takes more than a little run-in with a half ton of hamburger to do in a Tankersley."

She was right about that. He'd seen for himself nine years before just how tough, how resilient, how determined the Tankersleys could be, when he'd believed everything his new banking client had told him about their loan transactions. He'd helped one unscrupulous banker almost destroy them at that time. Almost. That was the operative word. And now in the intensity of the moment he had almost forgotten that the Tankersleys would probably never forgive him for his misguided zeal in that lawsuit, just as he had almost forgotten that Victoria Tankersley in no way resembled what he had always thought he wanted in a woman.

"I'd better be going then," he said, looking away from her but not before he had seen the small flare of hurt well up from the depths of her eyes.

"Sure," she said, struggling to sit up and wincing when she did so. "I know you're busy. I—I— Thanks for your help today."

He paused at the bedroom door, half turning, knowing he wanted to say something else but not knowing what. Once again their gazes locked; once again he felt the sweet ache of desire. "Take care," he said.

"Yeah." She gave him a cheeky grin, incongruous with the paleness of her face. "I think I'd better."

VICTORIA LISTENED until she heard Phil's footsteps leave the hall and cross the living room before she eased herself down on the bed, giving into aches that she would never have admitted to him.

"Wilcox," she murmured. He couldn't hear her. She didn't want him to hear her. She listened until she heard the back door close and his truck start up. "Just why *did* you come out here today?"

She fumbled with her clothes, and her hands came to rest on her bare flesh. He'd touched her. Had she betrayed to him how much his touch had affected her? She didn't think so. Once she had gotten over her initial shock, she'd done her best to hide her reaction. After all, he meant nothing by it. As he had so calmly informed her, he *had* to touch her.

She closed her eyes, digging at her forehead with her fingers. Oh, Lord, she had been alone too long if a man's—if *that* man's—impersonal touch could turn her into a quivering mass of overworked hormones.

Teenaged crush be damned. Her unreasonable sense of betrayal when he had represented the bank in the foreclosure be damned. He was Phil Wilcox. A man who probably only read law books. A man who wasn't interested in anything but his career and, on a superficial level only, his gentleman's ranch. A man who was probably no more sensitive than the football he had carried across the field when he was in college. And even if he was, and Victoria knew this was the bottom line, he was a man who could never be interested in her.

Chapter Three

"You feeling okay this morning, Vickie? You look a little peaked."

The sun was barely up, a pale blur in the ashen gray November sky, as her father backed the pickup truck up to the barn door where Victoria waited for him.

"Sure Pop," she told him. "I'm just having a little trouble getting started." That much, at least, was not a lie. After a night's troubled sleep, her bruised and battered muscles had set up a screaming protest at moving. For a while, she had been afraid that they wouldn't let her move.

When her father had returned to the house the day of her accident, he had been too preoccupied with a letter he'd just received from his brother Ted in New Mexico to notice anything different about her. By that night, when she thought more than once she had caught him studying her, she was moving in a pretty fair imitation of her normal actions. Now—she knew it always bothered him that she was the one who had to do the heavy work—now there was no way she would let him know that she felt even less able than he was to do what had to be done. Gritting her teeth, she scrambled up the narrow metal ladder to the barn loft.

UNLIKE THE MORNING BEFORE, Phil knew exactly why he turned up the Tankersleys' drive. He'd fought the idea half the night, since it first occurred to him, telling himself that it was not his business, not his problem. But he couldn't turn away from it. After what had happened to Victoria, and with Zack Tankersley in poor health, somebody was going to have to feed their cattle.

He parked near the brightly lighted kitchen and stepped from his truck. He didn't worry about being too early; he knew Tankersley was from the old school of ranching, a man who insisted on feeding his livestock each morning before he fed himself.

He heard the thunk of baled hay hitting metal and turned toward the barn. He recognized the battered truck parked beneath the loft doors from the sale barn. He almost didn't recognize the man standing beside it. He identified the thin, stooped man leaning on a cane only because he expected to see Zack Tankersley.

Well, he thought as another bale bounced into the truck, he'd wasted a trip. Obviously they had found a neighbor to help. He considered getting back in his truck and leaving, avoiding the problem of trying to explain his presence, when Tankersley turned and waved a beckoning arm. He saw the frown that crossed the man's face when he got close enough to be recognized, but he saved his words of explanation until he wouldn't have to shout them. Instead, he shrugged deeper in his jacket against the frigid morning wind and looked up toward the loft to see which of Tankersley's neighbors had relieved him of his self-imposed responsibility.

Victoria? She appeared in the loft doorway, lugging a bale of hay. Even from that distance, he saw beads of sweat on her upper lip and forehead as she swung her arms and released her burden into the bed of the waiting truck.

"What in the *hell* do you think you're doing?"

The roared words blasted over her as she tried to catch her breath. Phil? Here? *Why?* She recognized the voice, the tone, even the words, without looking, but she acknowledged him anyway. He stood next to the truck, his large frame radiating waves of anger, while her father stood beside him, slack-jawed with surprise.

"Wilcox," she said, leaning against the doorjamb, hiding the fight she was waging against the catch in her side and trying to hide her own surprise. "You are going to have to learn a new opening line."

"Get your—" He visibly controlled himself. "Get down here." Then, losing the battle for control, he roared, "Now!"

"Just a minute . . ." Pop began.

Victoria sighed in frustration. All she needed was for those two to get crossways with each other. "It's all right, Pop. Mr. Wilcox meant to say please." She nodded toward Phil. "Didn't you?"

Phil glanced from her to her father then back to her. "Yes," he said, not releasing but not voicing any of his anger. "I did."

Knowing she might as well go down and get whatever it was Phil had on his mind over with, she swung herself onto the ladder and began backing down. She felt a pair of large, strong hands close around her waist and winced at the pressure against her tightly wrapped ribs.

"Rib belt?" Phil whispered in her ear.

She cast a surreptitious glance toward her father. Had he heard? "Sshh!" she whispered.

He removed his hands from her waist, only to grasp her around her shoulders and beneath her knees, lift her from the ladder, and set her on her feet.

Zack leaned back against the truck, looking from one to the other of them. "Want to tell me what this is all about?" he asked.

"Victoria had an accident yesterday."

"Vickie." The dismay in Zack's voice could be heard. "Why didn't you say something?"

"There wasn't anything to say," she answered abruptly. She glanced at Phil, pleading with her eyes and hoping that Pop couldn't read her silent message. "It wasn't all that serious."

"Wilcox?"

Phil hesitated a second before turning back to Zack. "Maybe it wasn't," he said finally. "At least it wouldn't have been had it involved you or me." Victoria felt a warm rush of gratitude that he had included her father in the comment, gratitude that fled with Phil's next words. "But I don't think she should be lifting things or doing any hard work for the next several days."

Victoria saw pain welling up in her father's deep-set eyes. "You should have told me."

"Yeah. Well..." Maybe she should have told him. But what good would it have done? "Somebody has to feed the cattle."

"That's why I'm here. That is, Zack," Phil added, "unless you object."

The older man studied Phil, looked him up and down as though measuring him. Zack didn't smile; he gave no outward indication of where his thoughts had traveled, or why. "No," he said. "I don't object."

VICTORIA'S FATHER had remained silent. Of course, there hadn't been much time for talk until after the last trip had been made to the barn, the last herd had been fed, the last gate had been closed, and Phil had gratefully climbed into the warm cab of the truck with him for the return trip to the house.

"You want to tell me about that accident?" Zack asked over the combined roar of the truck's muffler and heater fan.

Phil stuffed his feet up under the heater vent as far as he could get them and slouched back in the seat. He ought to; if he left it to Victoria, she no doubt would play down her injuries out of concern for her father. "I don't think so."

"Were you with her?"

"Yes."

"Was it your fault?"

Phil glanced sharply at Zack. Was it his fault? He'd asked himself that question at least one hundred times. Given her attitude and his, could he have done anything to prevent what had happened? He didn't honestly know, and he couldn't honestly answer.

"I reckon not," Zack said when Phil remained silent. "Otherwise, you wouldn't have been out here this morning. But you didn't answer, so that leads me to believe that maybe you think that some way you were responsible.

"I don't know you very well, Wilcox," he went on. "I know *of* you, but you and I haven't had any business dealings for a long time."

Phil pulled his still-cold feet back from the heater and sat up. "I wondered when we'd get around to that," he said. Not only had he wondered when, he'd wondered how, because there was some serious unfinished business wrapped up in those few words.

"How old were you then? About thirty?"

"About," Phil said, wondering where this was leading.

"And you'd been in practice for a few years."

"A few."

"Long enough so that you should have been suspicious of that banker when he had all those pat answers."

Phil didn't squirm. He wanted to, but he held himself immobile. "Yeah."

"Just like I should have been suspicious when he asked me to sign those blank notes.... Hell!" Zack said, "we were blowin' and goin' so fast, sometimes I didn't have time to get to the bank. Cattle prices were high, and getting better. I was raking in money with every trade, turning around and putting it back into more cattle to trade, more equipment, more land. Fact is," he said, for the first time letting bitterness creep into his voice, "I trusted him, too."

Zack downshifted as he headed the truck up the hill toward the house. "I've got a bunch of regrets over that whole deal. One of them being that I didn't hire you before that banker had a chance to."

He parked the truck next to Phil's newer, flashier one, but made no move to kill the engine. Phil sat unmoving as he digested the older man's words. They didn't absolve him of the responsibility he felt for that long-distant travesty of justice, he didn't know if any-

thing ever would, but he knew now that at least *Zack*
Tankersley wasn't nursing a decade-old grudge.

"How about some breakfast?"

"No." Phil roused himself from his thoughts. Well-
intentioned or not, he'd intruded on these people long
enough, and he wasn't sure he wanted to see Victoria
again, not until he'd had more time to think. "No,
thanks."

Zack turned the key and killed the engine. "At least
come in for a cup of coffee. Your insides have got to
be as cold as your outside is."

Zack was right about that. "Okay," he agreed,
smiling. "But only one."

Phil's smile faded when he entered the warm kitchen
and saw what waited. He'd had the misguided notion
that Victoria would take advantage of the free time
he'd given her that morning to rest. Her? He should
have known better. He saw the evidence of a restricted diet, probably Zack's, on the table, but the
rest of the table groaned under the weight of enough
food for three hired hands.

"Looks good, Vickie. I'll be back in just a minute," Zack said as he shuffled from the kitchen.

"What's this?" Phil asked.

"Breakfast," Victoria told him. "It was the least I
could do." She handed him a bar of soap and a towel.
"You can wash up at the kitchen sink."

"You are the most—"

She whirled on him, eyes flashing. "I don't want to
hear it. And lower your voice! You did the neighborly
thing. I did the neighborly thing. Now wash up and eat
before it gets cold."

Rest? Victoria? She could barely walk, he noticed as
she carried a platter of ham to the table and sank onto

a chair, but would she go to bed? No. Not her. She made biscuits.

Suddenly he wanted her to rest. He wanted to see her relaxed and at ease. He wanted to see her smile. He wanted to see her with nothing to do but be waited upon and to enjoy herself. He threw the towel at the drain board and marched to the table, pulling out a chair and plopping his substantial body down next to her.

"I'm taking you out to dinner tonight."

She twisted her head around and looked at him as if he had just made an indecent proposal. "No."

"Yes."

She picked up the platter of biscuits and thrust it at him. "No!"

He took three of the biscuits before he set the platter down. "Do you want your father to know all the details of that 'not serious' accident?"

Her face blanched; her words came out in a rush of breath. "That's blackmail."

Phil paused in his reach for the eggs. "Yeah," he said, feeling surprised and inordinately pleased with himself, "it is." He flashed her a conqueror's smile. "Seven o'clock. Be ready."

"YOU WANT TO TELL ME about that accident?" Zack asked later that afternoon as she was trying to finish her paper for Monday's class.

"No," Victoria muttered. "I've got to get this done."

"It have anything to do with that other busted rail I found in the corral this morning?" he persisted.

"Oh, all right!" She pushed back from the typewriter, knowing she wouldn't get anything finished until she at least partially satisfied his curiosity and soothed his concern. As emotionlessly as possible she gave him a very brief, very edited version of the accident. "You know as well as I do that accidents happen," she said at the end of her account. "It could have been bad; but it wasn't. And I'm not hurt, not really, only a little bruised."

Her father's face creased in a deep frown. "But you could have been."

"Pop, we can't live on 'could have beens.'"

His frown eased. His eyes took on a narrow, speculative look that belied his rough appearance and gave evidence of a keen intelligence. "No?"

He gestured toward the typewriter. "More schoolwork?"

She smiled, glad that the inquisition was over. "A term paper."

"When are you going to finish up down there, Vickie? Next semester?"

"Yes," she said, sighing. "If everything goes according to plan."

He nodded, making no comment. She thought he was about to leave the room when he cocked his head. "What was Wilcox doing out here yesterday?"

She'd wondered the same thing, time after time during the night, and she hadn't found an answer. "Damned if I know."

"Vickie." She heard the reproval in his voice and remembered countless childhood lectures. *"Ladies don't talk like that."* Pain and unhappiness and frustration welled up within her. She could tell him some other things ladies didn't do. Ladies didn't wear boots permanently encrusted from wading through mud and cow manure; ladies didn't get up before dawn in freezing weather to toss sixty-five-pound bales of hay into a pickup truck and then toss them out to hungry cattle; ladies didn't ruin their nails and rip their hands open stretching barbed wire fence.

Not fair! Not fair, she told herself, trying to calm her frustration before she said any of those things. It simply was not fair to him. He couldn't do anything about his health. And she loved ranch life, she really did. She loved the cattle; she loved the beauty of the land. She didn't even mind the work; not really. It was just that there was so much of it.

"So?" her father asked again. "Why was he here?"

"I don't know," she told him, once again caught in that question. "He never got around to telling me. Must not have been very important."

ANGELA WAS IN the living room when Phil got home, draped over a chair in front of the blaring television, schoolbooks spread in a wide circle around her. Gone was the would-be sophisticate of Friday night. She was wearing a gray football practice jersey, which would have been loose on him even with shoulder pads, and hot-pink sweatpants with a pair of his white boot socks pulled up over them.

Phil postponed his intended trip to the coffeepot long enough to detour through the living room, where he turned down the volume on the television and greeted his daughter.

"Mmmm," she said in response, obviously lost deep in thought. He had reached the kitchen door before she spoke coherent words, calling out so that he heard her across the dining room. "Is thirty-five too old for you?"

He backtracked to the living room doorway. "What?"

"Thirty-five? Is that too old for you? I know some men like younger women, so I thought I'd better check."

"Angela, what are you talking about?"

"She fits all the requirements. Well almost all of them. She's five nine. I couldn't get her weight, but she wears a size twelve. She's a C.P.A., so that means she has a degree and has to have some smarts. Not a blonde, though. Not quite. She has light brown hair. I'm sorry about that, but after all, I've only had today to work on it."

"Angela," he repeated steadily, "what are you talking about?"

She looked up at him and grinned, a disarming, alarm-sounding grin. "Maxine's Aunt Ingrid. She's coming to visit them over Thanksgiving."

"No." He turned on his heel and headed back toward the kitchen.

"Da-ad." He heard her scrambling from the chair and following him. "You can't just reject her outright. I mean you're going to have to help me with this. At least look at her picture."

"No," he repeated. He stopped at the kitchen door and whirled to face her. She skidded to a stop inches away. "You asked for a picture of her?"

"Well. No. Not yet . . ."

"But you were going to?"

"Well . . ."

"How many people have you told about your plan to . . ." God! He couldn't believe this. He thought he'd persuaded her to drop her wild idea.

"Nobody. Yet."

Another tack. That was obviously what he needed. "How would you like for me to find you a boyfriend?" he asked with more patience than he felt.

"Well . . . I guess if he were really dreamy, I'd like it just fine."

Wrong tack. "How would you like it if I went to the school and announced that I was going to have to find you a boyfriend because you couldn't do it on your own?"

Her eyes widened and her mouth opened once, twice, gasping before she forced out the words. "You wouldn't!"

"No," he told her. "And you won't either."

She took a deep breath and let it out. "Oh. I get the picture." She backed away from him, holding up her hands and nodding in what he hoped was understanding. It wasn't. She made that clear with her next words. "Discretion. I can handle that. Sure. Discretion."

Phil slammed through the kitchen door, letting it swing shut behind him. Women! Had some sanity-destroying virus attacked the entire female sex? He snatched a coffee cup from the cabinet, filled it and leaned back against the counter shaking his head. Maybe that bug had infected him, too, because while his daughter was in the next room conspiring to find him a tall, blond beauty, all he could think about, all he wanted to think about was Victoria Tankersley.

PITCHLYN COUNTY, Oklahoma, on a Sunday night didn't offer much in the way of restaurant selection, and since Styx Switch, the county seat, was the only area within reasonable distance that offered any variety, that's where they were, sitting in the dimly lighted back dining room of the town's one hotel. Phil had picked her up promptly at seven, driving a big, comfortable Oldsmobile and wearing slacks and a cable-knit sweater over a pale blue shirt.

He had glanced at the jeans and boots Victoria had defiantly chosen to wear, but he hadn't said anything about them. He hadn't said much of anything, she realized as she handed the menu to the waitress after Phil had placed their orders.

"Relax," he said.

Relax? She had never been able to relax in his presence, and she certainly couldn't now, after he had touched her, after her mind and body had taken the sensations and twisted them into something he had never intended. "Relax?"

"Yes. One usually does on a date."

"This isn't a date," she said, reminding him, reminding herself. "This is a payoff."

He closed his eyes for a moment, shuttering his expression, let out a deep breath and picked up his coffee cup. "Right," he said. "So in compliance with that payoff, will you at least try to relax?"

What did he want with her? What other "compliance" was he going to come up with? Maybe a discreet little trip into a hotel room?

"Victoria."

She looked across the table and noticed for the first time that Phil looked tired. His beautiful gray eyes, so startlingly different in color from what she expected with his rich, red hair, looked frustrated.

"This has gone on long enough," he said. "I'm not going to tell your father anything you don't want me to. I had thought—I had hoped that we could spend some time together, enjoy a meal together. That's all. Is that so wrong?"

Was it? Not when he phrased it like that. She smiled ruefully and caught a glimpse of an answering grin glimmering through his red beard and mustache. She fought a vagrant urge to touch his beard, to trace her finger along the lips now tilted so appealingly. "Your technique has a lot in common with a bulldozer," she said.

"Would anything else have worked?"

"Probably not," she admitted.

Surprising herself, Victoria did relax. Phil could be charming company; he proved that to her, even though she suspected he was deliberately trying to. She found herself sharing impersonal anecdotes with him, laughing with him, enjoying being with him. Until the waitress cleared away their plates and refilled their coffee cups. Phil waited until the woman left the table, then drawing his finger along the edge of his cup, looked over at her.

"How long have you been home?"

Victoria hesitated as she reached for her cup, then picked it up. "Almost forever," she said. "I had to go back to school to take care of things, but I came home as soon as I could, and I've been here ever since."

"Why didn't I know?"

She bit back a bitter answer. She hadn't hidden from him. She hadn't hidden from anyone. And he seemed genuinely puzzled. "I don't know, Phil. Maybe—maybe it's because it's easier for me to do what shopping I have to do in the south end of the county. I seldom come into Hillsboro, almost never as far north as Styx Switch."

He studied her for a moment, as though not satisfied with her answer. "What about graduate school? Your plans for teaching?"

He was treading on painful subjects, but she tried not to let it show. "Graduate school requires money," she said lightly. "There wasn't an abundance of that left. And college-level teaching requires graduate school. End of story."

"Not quite," he persisted, and she wondered why it seemed so important to him. Guilt over his part of it? Maybe, but she wasn't sure that was all of it. "What about the man who put that engagement ring on your hand?"

Her hand trembled when she replaced her coffee cup. It had been visible to her; Phil must have seen it. She didn't owe him an answer. In spite of his denial, this evening was a blackmail payoff. All she owed him was her presence. But as she looked across the table at him watching her patiently, intently, she realized that she did want to answer.

"Brad," she said, wishing she smoked so that she would have something to do with her hands. She folded them together and held them tightly in her lap. "Brad was a graduate student at Yale. His sister was my roommate. We had our future all planned out. Teaching positions at the same university—his in history, mine in literature. A white federal-styled house on a tree-lined street. Three bright, beautiful, well-behaved children. A dog that would stay outside—wouldn't want an animal destroying the Sheraton and Hepplewhite. A paneled library. Scholarly friends. And talented students, who sat at our feet eager to glean any words of wisdom we let drop."

Her hands, still clenched together, had migrated to the tabletop. Phil squeezed them gently and covered both of them with one of his. "What happened?" he prompted in a low voice.

She tried to smile and failed miserably. "I'd told Leah, Brad's sister, several stories about the ranch, but I guess her hearing was as selective as my telling." She looked across the table at Phil and saw nothing but understanding and concern in his eyes. "Brad came to see me after I came home. We were down to what we have now, about a thousand acres. I guess to someone who measures land in twenty-five-acre Long Island estates or Manhattan real estate, that must have sounded like a lot of land. I think he had this picture in his mind of me getting up every morning, dressing in my Dale Evans costume, and going out to give daily work assignments to the Sons of the Pioneers.

"When he found out that there were no 'Sons of the Pioneers,' that I did the chores, when he learned how little income and how much work a thousand-acre hill-country ranch actually produces, when he mired his Gucci loafers in the barn lot, the reality was too much for him. I couldn't leave at the time. He wouldn't give up his dream to join me, especially after he had seen me in my natural setting, and I—" her voice threatened to break, but she refused to let it "—and I had destroyed his image of me."

Phil lowered his head, shaking it slowly from side to side before he raised it once again to meet her eyes. "Oh, Victoria," he said softly, so softly she barely heard him. "I am so sorry."

"I was, too," she told him, straightening her shoulders, tightening her hold on her wayward emotions and pushing her memories to the past, where they belonged. "At the time."

Phil seemed reluctant to release her hand, but he did so, fumbling for the check and his wallet with an uncharacteristic lack of grace, remaining silent until they reached the solitude inside his car. There he turned to her, but instead of speaking, he shook his head, returned his attention to the car, started it and spun out onto the highway, heading south toward their homes.

Victoria watched him silently; she didn't want to, but she couldn't force her eyes to turn from the sight of his rigidly held massive shoulders, the smooth unyielding column of his neck rising to the luxuriant beard that hid his jaw. Once again she fought the impulse to raise her fingers to that beard, to see for herself if it felt as silkily erotic as it looked.

"You never remarried," she said to break the silence, to break her train of thought.

The question required no answer; Phil gave none.

"The girls in my high school graduating class used to make bets on who would catch you," she persisted. "Over half of them wanted you to wait long enough for it to be one of them." She didn't tell him that she had once belonged to that majority.

Phil laughed harshly and muttered into the darkness in the car, "Maybe someday they'll erect a plaque in my honor."

"What?"

"Never mind," he told her, but her words, or his thoughts, had had the effect she desired. His shoulders lost some of their rigidity; his head tilted slightly on the column of his neck.

"What was she like?" Victoria asked softly, wanting to know about the woman he had married, the woman he had not found anyone to replace. "Your wife?"

Phil's mouth narrowed into a tight slash before he apparently decided to answer her. "Beautiful," he said tersely. "Alluringly feminine. Tall. Leggy."

With each of his words, with the pictures they invoked, Victoria felt herself being pushed away from him. Of course his wife would have been beautiful, would have been all the things Victoria was not.

"Do you know the Nichols family?" Phil asked in what Victoria recognized and resented as an abrupt change of subject. He hadn't shown any reluctance in pushing her for answers to very personal questions, but it didn't appear that his need for verbal intimacy ran in both directions.

"I don't know them." She spoke just as tersely as he had a moment before. "But I know *of* them. I don't suppose there are many people in this part of the state who don't know who David Nichols is."

"Only it wasn't David who was the big name, then," Phil said. "It was his father, my uncle Jake. My wife Gloria had heard of him, too. And, of course, I was making quite a name for myself at that time. Quarterback for the Oklahoma Sooners in my junior year. A lot of talk about being a shoo-in for the Heisman Trophy my senior year. It was a match made in heaven. Until Gloria finally realized what I had never made any secret of, that all the money was on Uncle Jake's side of the family, and I had no intention of playing pro football, that the only reason I played at all was because I needed the scholarship. She didn't wait around to see what I'd do with my future. Neither Angela nor I was sufficient incentive for her to suffer through my three years of law school and the financial insecurity of building a small-town law practice.''

"Oh," Victoria said in a small voice.

"Yeah," Phil told her, and in his voice she heard an echo of her own dismay. "Oh."

The house was dark when Phil parked his car near her kitchen door. He opened his door and got out without any pretext of detaining her, but before she could release her seat belt and open her door, he had walked around the car and opened it for her. He walked with her to the back porch, not touching her, not speaking.

"Victoria." She stopped on the first step, turning in surprise at the hesitancy in his voice. "I want to see you again."

"Phil, I . . ." Dragging up old memories couldn't have been any less painful for him than it had been for her. "What good would it do?"

"We could start over," he told her. His lips curved in an appealing smile. "Without coercion. Who knows, we might even discover that we like each other."

Against her will, she felt herself warming to his smile. They might discover that after all. In the past three days she had already discovered a lot about him: that he wasn't the ogre she had tried for so long to imagine him; that her body, if not her heart, was more drawn to him now than she had been in her adolescent crush.

"Tomorrow night?" he asked.

Such a simple question, she thought, but it shattered the mood. "I can't."

He absorbed her answer for a moment. "Then the next night."

"I can't." She reached out and touched his shoulder, knowing she shouldn't, but unable to deny herself this one moment of contact as she realized that for the next several months she had no time in her life for Phil Wilcox, she had no time in her life for anything but what was already mapped out. "I'm sorry, Phil," she told him, "but I really can't see you again. I already have plans."

She should have told him what those plans were. Victoria knew that, but she couldn't. Part of her reluctance, she told herself, was for his sake. He had seemed genuinely sorry when he learned that she had had to give up her dreams of graduate school. Part of it, she admitted, was for herself; she had been so confident in the past, so sure of her future, that she couldn't—just couldn't—admit to this man that *none* of it had come to be, not even the degree in literature that he assumed she had completed.

"I see," he said, and Victoria knew from the coldness in his voice and the tension in his body that he didn't "see" at all.

"And if I hadn't forced the issue, you wouldn't have gone out with me tonight, would you?"

Would she have? Victoria knew she wanted to, but would she actually have said yes without his ridiculous threat? "Phil, I . . ."

As they stood facing each other in the darkness, Victoria felt the weight of another misunderstanding lodging itself between them but was powerless to do anything about it.

"Oh, hell," Phil muttered, lifting his hands to clasp her shoulders. "You already hate me. This can't make it any worse."

There was nothing punishing about his kiss. Victoria realized that immediately through the emotional armor she had erected to fight off his assault. She felt the brush of his beard on her face, soft, silky as she had imagined, and then his lips on hers, firm, demanding, possessive, but not in her wildest flights of imagination could she ever describe them as punishing. And not in her wildest flight of fancy could she imagine not responding to him and to the message he was silently communicating. I am man. You are woman. I want you. Feel! Feel what pleasure we can share.

She swayed forward, opening her mouth to the welcomed invasion of his, and felt his arms go around her, drawing her still closer, until her breasts, tinglingly alive and aware of him, were flattened against his chest. She lifted her hands to his head and as she pulled his head closer to hers, she found his hair as silky and inviting as his beard. As she slanted her mouth to be more open to his, she lost herself in the warmth of him, in the warmth of sensations spreading through her, urging her closer and closer. As though he felt the same urging, he spread his hands on her back, tightening his grasp on her and lifting her against him. She felt a moan building within her that escaped softly into the warm velvet of his mouth as she felt his waiting need. But when his hands shifted lower, possessively, to her sore ribs, reality took over.

Phil released her instantly. Not so quickly, he drew her hands from his neck and stepped back from her. "I'm sorry," he said, not looking at her.

"Phil?" Her voice was thick, her thoughts confused.

"I'm sorry," he repeated. "I didn't mean to hurt you. But intentions don't always count, do they?"

She reached out to him, but he took another step back. "I'll get out of your life. That's what you've been trying to tell me since I stumbled back into it." He looked at her hand, still outstretched toward him, and then at her face. "Goodbye, Victoria," he said gently after long, silent seconds. "Take care of yourself."

She wanted to call him back, wanted to tell him that the last thing she wanted was for him to get out of her life, but what did she have to offer him? Not even her time. She stood on the porch until his taillights disappeared below the crest of the hill, hugging her arms, aware once again of the chilly November night, and feeling more alone than she had ever felt in her life. Then, lifting her chin and squaring her shoulders in stubborn defiance, she entered the dark house. *Take care of herself?* Sure. She could do that. She'd had a lot of practice.

Chapter Four

Harbingers of spring, Phil's sister Eunice had once called the hibiscus now poking their blue and purple flowered heads out of the slightly shaggy beds bordering his wraparound porch. As if he needed any more harbingers, he had teased her; the new calf crop and the myriad difficulties his clients found themselves in with the first hint of warm weather were warning enough that a change was coming.

"Don't be bullheaded, Phil," Eunice told him. "You may want to live in a scruffy bachelor's quarters, but your daughter deserves better. Call it an early Christmas present or a late birthday present, but you are getting flowers."

Money had still been tight for Eunice that year, but her pride had always been as fierce as his. She'd gathered up the family clan, and for a weekend had blitzed his yard, weeding, chopping and planting.

He thought he'd been salvaging Eunice's pride by letting her landscape his yard. Maybe he had. But as he stepped up onto the porch that February day and turned to look over the yard, he knew she had given him more than a weekend of labor and a boxful of plants. She'd given him a visible reminder of how

much love his family had shared while he was growing up and of how far they had come in the succeed-
ing years. Eunice was financially secure now. Few
major crises marred her life; several months had
passed since the last minor one. Success hadn't come
easily for her; too few things in her life had. But she
had been right about it coming. For a kid sister, she
had been right about a remarkable number of things.
But not, he thought, about him wanting to live in a
bachelor's quarters, scruffy or otherwise.

Pride. It was a strange and awesome thing. He remembered how pride had stiffened Eunice's back and
darkened her eyes as she told him that for *once* she was
doing something for *him*. She'd come by it honestly.
A streak of pride a mile wide ran through the entire
family. Wounded pride was what had made him leave
Victoria that night without pressing for answers he
now knew—that she was up to her neck in medical
bills, work and school.

Why hadn't he known before? The explanation
Victoria had given him was only partially valid. The
Ouachita Mountains that covered the southeastern
part of Pitchlyn County and thrust out to divide the
north half of the county from the south had once been
a very real barrier to communication and transporta-
tion. But he had family south of the outthrust. His
cousin David lived there, and Eunice had an outlet
store almost at the southern county line. But then,
neither David nor Eunice would want to remind him
of that fiasco with the Tankersleys. Both of them were
conscious of the Wilcox pride.

And pride wasn't limited to their family. After Victoria's accident, after their one disastrous date, Phil
had sent Tom Jenkins, one of his ranch hands, out to

the Tankersley place to help with the feeding and whatever else needed to be done. Victoria had accepted that help for two weeks, a sure sign that it had been necessary, and then had sent Tom back to Phil with a sealed envelope containing a polite thank you and a check reimbursing him for the man's wages. Phil hadn't wanted to take her money; he knew she probably couldn't afford it. But her pride was one of the few things she had left. He had cashed the check. And he had spent the last three months trying to convince himself that he was doing the right thing by staying out of her life.

He felt a wry smile twisting his mouth. If Angela only knew. But she didn't. And if he had anything to say about it, she wouldn't. Her matchmaking attempts were driving him crazy. He had to talk to her about them. He had decided the time wouldn't get any better and for most of the afternoon had gone over what he could say to stop her scheming.

Something was wrong. Phil knew that the moment he opened the door, but it was another moment before he identified what. Silence. No blast of rock music greeted him as he stepped into the hallway. No television blared from the living room. "Angela?" No cheerful voice greeted him.

"Angela?" he repeated, stepping into the living room. She was there in her favorite position, draped crossways over the arms of his chair, and in her favorite disreputable old sweats, with her flaming red hair caught high in a ponytail. One hand gripped a pencil protruding from the side of her mouth, the other, a slender book pressed against her upraised knees.

"Angela," he said again, knowing she probably hadn't heard him come in.

"Mmm," came the muffled greeting from around the pencil.

There was no need to hide his smile at her rapt concentration; she wouldn't see it. "Any messages?"

She loosed her grip on the pencil long enough to wave vaguely in the direction of the desk in the alcove of the bay window. Grinning openly, Phil walked to the desk and riffled through the scrawled message sheets. Nothing too important, although there were several. One of the disadvantages of being a small-town attorney, or advantages, depending on his frame of mind and what he was trying to do, was that everyone knew where to find him, before, during or after office hours. He glanced at the telephone, receiver off the hook and lying upended on the desk. For a moment he considered replacing it, then looked back at his daughter who was once again caught up in whatever she was studying.

"Heavy test coming up?" he prompted.

She glanced up at him, looking at him for the first time, and her face softened in a smile. "Something like that. Do you mind?"

"No. Of course not." But he might as well have saved his breath. She was back in the book before he spoke.

Having decided to talk to her this evening, Phil was at a loss as to how to start. He knew any conversation would take several minutes, and he wanted to get it over with before the usual Friday crowd of young people descended on the house to pick her up. "No date tonight?"

"Mmm? No. Sorry, Dad. I just didn't have time this week. You'll have to fend for yourself."

"Thank God," he murmured.

"What?" came her muffled response.

"Nothing," he said quickly.

Phil shook his head. The only way his daughter could be less present was if she were physically not there. Maybe the talk wouldn't be necessary. At last something had detoured her from what had seemed to be her single-minded goal. He reached for the telephone receiver, then left it where it was and made his way into the kitchen, to the waiting coffeepot.

Fend for himself. He wondered if Angela knew how good that sounded to him after weeks of fending off her matchmaking efforts, or, to keep some semblance of peace in the family, going along with them to a limited degree. He had been out with Maxine's Aunt Ingrid, with Jessica's cousin Louise, with Angela's math teacher's younger sister, as well as various other visiting friends and relatives of friends whom Angela had managed to ferret out and present to him as "perfect" for him. Lovely ladies. Most of them. And all of them with one or two of the characteristics on that insane list he had been guilty of helping draft.

And none of the women had done one thing to help erase the memory of Victoria Tankersley's expressive black eyes flashing with anger or hooded with need, to erase the memory of the pride he had felt watching her competently perform tasks, to erase the memory of how good, and how right, she had felt in his arms.

Fend for himself. He could call her. Three months had passed. Surely there had been some improvement in her circumstances. "Fool, Wilcox," he told himself. "The woman doesn't have time for you. She made that abundantly clear." And even if she did have the time, why would she want to spend it with him?

"AFTERNOON, VICTORIA."

"Good afternoon, Mr. Richards," Victoria said, smiling as she surrendered the empty prescription bottles to the stately, white-haired pharmacist on the other side of the tall counter. Behind his back, he was referred to as Doc, but to his face, at least to anyone under the age of fifty, he was always Mr. Richards.

He studied the bottles, frowned slightly, and smiled at her. "How's Zack doing?"

"Pop's fine," she told him, going through the familiar ritual.

"Heard you were teaching here in town."

"Student teaching," she amended. "Freshman and sophomore grammar." Not literature as she had hoped. Then, grinning, she repeated what a professor had once said in one of her grammar classes. "It's a dirty job, but someone's got to do it."

He gave a full-throated roar of laughter. "Don't I know it. Kids! Sometimes I have to ask them three or four times what they want before I can understand them. You'd think they were speaking another language."

She had heard a variation of this speech from him for as long as she could remember, and he required no response from her but an attentive expression and a sparkle of understanding in her eyes.

"Abbie's grandson is in one of your classes," he went on. "She says you're doing him a world of good. Says he doesn't swear nearly as much now."

Victoria chuckled. Jimmie Foresman wasn't watching his language because of anything she had done but because Lydia Benton, a freshman blond bombshell who could easily pass for a senior, had informed him that if he was too lazy to learn anything other than those dumb old tacky words that any tobacco-chewing, rednecked hick already knew, she guessed she just wouldn't have time for him. Victoria thought Lydia had been a little tough on him, but she appreciated any and all help she could get.

Doc glanced back at the prescription bottles. "I've got a couple of orders ahead of these. If you need to get on home, I can fill them and hold them for you until tomorrow."

She needed to get home, but for the first time in months, she wasn't in a great hurry. She shook her head. "Thanks, anyway, but I'll wait."

The front of the drugstore was devoted to a soda fountain. The building had been constructed just after statehood, and the fountain had ruled supreme in downtown Hillsboro, with only minor modifications since that time. Victoria wandered toward the front of the store. The stools at the fountain had given way to two rows of Formica-topped, low-backed vinyl-covered booths, but the cherry and marble back bar was original. The high, decorative tin ceiling was original, and, some said, so was Abigail Foresman, who admitted to more than thirty-five years of measuring coke syrup, carbonated water and ice cream for the generations of young people who had always flocked to her counter.

"Cherry-lime phosphate?" Abigail asked when Victoria approached the counter.

Victoria smiled. This particular concoction had been invented by Doc's dad and touted for miles around as a cure for scurvy. The recipe persisted through the years, gaining and losing popularity, but remaining one of the staples of the fountain. "A large one."

She glanced around the room. She'd stayed after school for her weekly planning conference and most of the young people had already gone home since it was late. Only one table of high-spirited, laughing kids remained. As she accepted the glass from Abigail, sipping the sweet-tart concoction and feeling the fizz of carbonation tickling her nose, they rose and good-naturedly jostled their way out the door, leaving her alone in the time warp of Richards' Drug Store.

Not quite alone. She noticed the bright red head in a booth that had been hidden from her view before. Hair like that had to belong to a Wilcox, and when the girl in the booth shifted and moved her head slightly, Victoria recognized Phil's daughter.

Victoria had seen Angela around the high school several times. She was outgoing, effervescent. But the Angela Wilcox sitting alone in a back booth of Richards' Drugstore was anything but bubbly. Troubled would be a better description, if Victoria had to pin it down to one word.

Leave it alone, she told herself. Angela wasn't her problem. She wasn't in any of her classes. And Victoria didn't have the time or energy to take on anyone else's problems.

She brought herself up with a quick, sharp oath. When she didn't have time for another human being's pain, then it was past time for her to quit pretending to belong to the same race. She started back toward the booth.

Why? she asked herself, the thought unbidden and unwelcome. *Because she's someone who looks like she needs help? Or because she's Phil's daughter?*

Victoria paused. Phil had nothing to do with this. He was just someone who had reentered her life at a very trying time for her, had shown her concern and kindness and then had gone on his way after an ungracious shove from her. Wasn't he?

Angela frowned; a vertical line creased her forehead, and she twisted her mouth. Victoria pushed her thoughts away and stepped to the side of the booth. "Angela? Are you all right?"

Angela looked up at her. Victoria saw recognition in her eyes before the girl grimaced wryly and pushed the literature book and the smaller volume it had concealed to one side. "Am I that obvious?"

Victoria shook her head and glanced questioningly at the vacant side of the booth.

"Sure," Angela said. Then, apparently remembering her manners and that she was talking to a teacher, added. "Please, Miss Tankersley. Sit down."

Victoria slid into the booth, took another sip from her phosphate, and then casually traced her finger around the perimeter of the slender volume that lay in the center of the table. She recognized the book as a stage edition of *Romeo and Juliet*, which had been selected for the all-school play that spring, and began to suspect the reason for Angela's preoccupation. "Tryouts are Friday, aren't they?" Victoria asked.

Angela tensed, then relaxed. "I don't know why I'm keeping it such a secret. I mean, everybody's going to know when I get up there and make a big fool of myself, anyway."

Victoria hesitated. Adolescent egos could be so fragile if not handled tenderly. "Will you?" she asked. "Make a fool of yourself?"

Angela sighed. "I don't know. I'm good. At least I think I am. I've been reading the part into a tape recorder at home, and it sounds—well, I mean, it doesn't sound like my voice, but it does sound pretty good."

"Have you read for anyone?"

Angela shook her head. "Who? Dad, maybe. He likes Shakespeare. But he has a habit of thinking that anything I do is a little better than it really is." She grinned wryly. "Or a little worse. Other than him, or maybe Uncle Ben, who's almost as bad as he is about me, I can't think of anyone else." She paused, studying Victoria, then stumbled ahead. "Would you—I mean, you've studied literature. Would you listen to me?"

While Victoria sat quite still, adjusting to the fact that Phil liked Shakespeare, to the glimpse of family unity that Angela had just given her, and wondering how she had gotten herself into this particular mess, Angela continued. "I want you to be honest with me, not just pat me on the head and tell me I did fine. I mean, I really want to know. Would you do that for me? Please."

Victoria felt helpless in the face of such earnest pleading. If Angela showed no talent or understanding of the part, there ought to be some tactful way to encourage further study; if she did—she needed support now. Victoria nodded her head.

"Great!" Angela relaxed with an enormous smile and grabbed for the playbook. "Just a short speech," she said, riffling through the pages then handing the book to Victoria. "It's one of my favorites."

Victoria glanced at the selection. Not the balcony scene as she had expected, but a scene from Act Four, where Juliet begs Friar Lawrence to help her escape from the marriage her family has planned for her, or to help her kill herself.

Angela closed her eyes for a moment, took two deep breaths, and began to speak in a soft, low voice. The timeless words carried a hint more melodrama than a seasoned actress would have given them, but given Angela's age, and Juliet's, the tone was understandable. In seconds Victoria forgot she was listening to a young girl trying out for a school play and found herself in the Friar's cell with a pain-filled and passionate young woman. When Angela fell quiet, Victoria opened her eyes, surprised for a moment to find herself back in Richards' Drugstore. She felt moisture in her eyes, and when she looked across the table, she saw an answering glimmer of moisture in Angela's. She swallowed once, channeling her energy into speaking. "You're good."

Angela's whoop of triumph caused Doc to look up from the prescription counter, smile resignedly and shake his head at Victoria.

"I made you cry," Angela said with wonder in her voice. "I made you cry."

Victoria grabbed a paper napkin from the dispenser and dabbed at her eyes. "Yes."

"Oh, boy," Angela said. "Oh, boy." A frown darkened her face and she fell unexpectedly quiet. "Now I just have one other problem." She propped her elbows on the table and leaned across toward Victoria. "I read, or maybe I heard that in Hollywood, if they have a really short leading man, they'll stand him on a box and just do close-ups, or maybe make the villain stand in a trench. I mean, it's done out there, so there ought to be some way to do it on the stage, shouldn't there?"

"Your height," Victoria said, brought back to reality with a resounding thud. "You're beautiful, Angela," she said earnestly. "Some women would kill for your height."

"Yeah. Well. Thanks," the girl said, acknowledging the compliment and dismissing it. "But those women aren't trying out for Juliet in a high school play."

No, they weren't. And a six-foot-tall Juliet posed a lot of problems for a small drama department. "You could be so good they'll forget how tall you are," Victoria offered.

"Could I? Do you really think so?"

"In New York, maybe. In Hillsboro, Oklahoma... I don't know," Victoria told her honestly. "But if you want to try, if you really want to try, knowing there can be no promises, I'll do everything I can to help you."

Angela reached across the table and grasped Victoria's hand, then dropped it abruptly. "I want this. I want it so much I can taste it. I want it so much I can't sleep, and I can't think about anything else. I know about 'no promises', Miss Tankersley. This is something I have to do."

Victoria saw Doc waving a small white sack at her and nodded her understanding to him. "Do you know where I live?" she asked Angela, knowing she shouldn't, and knowing there was no way she could not do this.

"Kind of."

Quickly, before she could talk herself into changing her mind, Victoria sketched a map on a napkin and handed it across the table. "I have to go home now. Give me a couple of hours to take care of some chores and then, if you want, come on out and we'll get started today."

PHIL NOTICED a difference in Angela Monday evening. After an entire weekend of watching her dogged concentration, he had become concerned about her, but at dinner that night, though preoccupied, she was at least present in spirit as well as body. Before going to bed, he passed her bedroom on the way to his. Through the open door, he saw her bent over her small drafting table, surrounded by discarded sketches and swatches of fabric. A set of headphones was clamped securely to her ears, and her lips were moving silently. Whatever was troubling her, he decided, she was working through it, and he knew his daughter well enough to know that she would eventually bring it to him.

On Tuesday night he heard the electric whir of her sewing machine and looked in to see her, headphones firmly in place, listening and sewing. She noticed him and nodded in his direction, then went back to her work.

By Thursday his curiosity, and concern, won out over his attempts to let Angela work through whatever was going on. He returned home a little later than usual to find the house as quiet as it had been for a week. No loud music. No television. No hordes of young people. No conversations tying up the telephone for hours. Neither Maxine nor Jessica had been out to the house, and Angela had shown no interest in visiting either of them.

He found Angela in the living room, her giant economy-sized sewing basket at her feet, doing some handwork on a colorful, seemingly shapeless bundle of fabric in her lap and for once not deafened by headphones. He pulled the desk chair near her, straddled it and leaned forward, resting his elbows on the back of the chair, as he looked down on the riotous hair and slender figure of the girl he wasn't at all sure he knew.

"New creation?" he asked.

She glanced up, smiled in the maddeningly absent way she had all week. "Mmm," she said and bent back to her sewing.

Phil scratched distractedly at his beard, wondering what to do next. Getting his daughter to talk to him had never been a problem before.

Angela looked up again, seeming puzzled that he was still there. "Do you want something, Dad?"

"Yes," he said, deciding that was as good an opening as he was going to get. "Angela, are you—" What? "Are you having problems at school?"

Her eyes widened at the question, but she shook her head slowly.

"Did you have a—a fight with Maxine and Jessica?"

Again she shook her head.

"A new boyfriend? Someone I don't know about?"

"No," she told him, but the word came out more as a question.

"Then what is it?" he asked, exasperation overruling tact. "You're troubled about something."

"Oh," she said, understanding lighting her eyes. "No. I was. Troubled, I mean. But I'm not now." She fumbled beneath the fabric in her lap and pulled out a small book and handed it to him. "I'm trying out for the part of Juliet in the school play tomorrow."

While Phil glanced at the cover of the playbook and then back toward her, Angela shook out the fabric and held it up for his inspection. "Does it look properly Elizabethan inspired?" she asked. "I'm doing my best to stack the odds in my favor."

"Tryouts," Phil said, staring at the street-length dress. "School play. It's—" he focused his attention on his daughter "—beautiful. I didn't know you were interested in acting."

"It's never seemed a viable option before," she told him.

Viable option. Phil felt the taste of the formal phrasing in his mouth but stopped himself before repeating it. Acting and legalese. Maybe he didn't know her as well as he had thought. "And now it is?"

She nodded. "Well, maybe not in high school. But with this—" She folded the dress carefully and placed it in her lap. "And with the help one of the teachers has been giving me, it might be. At least I'll know I gave it my best effort. And at least I have some idea of what else I want to study in college." She grinned up at him. "You need to meet this teacher, Dad. She—"

Phil threw his hands up in a defensive gesture. He had wanted his daughter returned to normal. Too bad he had forgotten for a moment what normal meant to her these days.

Angela's grin faded. Her gray eyes, so similar to his and yet so different, narrowed in study of him. Then she shook her head. "Nope. Not that way," she told him. "She's a super person, but she's just not your type."

VICTORIA EASED into the back of the school auditorium Friday afternoon and quietly made her way toward the stage where a small group of students clustered around Joan Bailey, the drama teacher. She spotted Angela immediately, standing a head taller than anyone else there, and groaned silently. Where were the jocks when you really needed them? But she knew. Not one of the football or basketball players would be caught dead prancing across the stage in a pair of tights.

Victoria had tried to talk herself out of attending the auditions. She'd given Angela all the time she could spare and all the help she could offer in the past week, suffering silently through the innocent anecdotes about her family and her father, which Angela seemed incapable of not telling. Forgetting that the girl was Phil's daughter had been impossible, except when she was in the role of Juliet, and Victoria had looked toward the end of her tutoring sessions with mixed feelings.

"All right," Joan called out, clapping her hands together sharply. "Let's get this started. Does everybody have a script?"

Victoria sank into an aisle seat as Joan began organizing the readings. Those for Juliet would be first, understandably, considering the number of females who wanted the lead. Most of them, she realized as the readings dragged on, hadn't a remote chance of getting it.

Finally it was Angela's turn. Victoria watched as she mounted the steps and took a position center stage. Good stage presence, Victoria noted, and then smiled as she realized Angela was wearing something most students would consider outlandishly stylish but that had a definite Elizabethan air.

The speech for the readings was from the balcony scene, and Victoria had heard it given that day in variations of fair, bad and worse. But no one in that auditorium, with the exception of Joan Bailey and herself, had ever heard it given better than Angela's reading. She recognized the dazed expression on Joan's face when Angela finished. She was sure she had worn the same expression the first time she heard the girl read. Joan gathered her senses, glanced at the playbook, and smiled weakly. "Thank you." She looked down at the list on her clipboard and cleared her throat. "Lydia Benton?"

Angela spotted Victoria as she left the stage and winked at her. Victoria gave the girl a thumbs up signal, surprised when Angela walked over and scooted into the seat next to hers.

"Is it bad luck to be proud of your reading?" Angela whispered.

Victoria shook her head. "Not one like that."

They both fell silent as Lydia began her reading. A petite blonde, Lydia had blossomed physically in her first year in high school, so much so that she was the envy of most of the girls in her class. Her reading was adequate. More than adequate, Victoria amended. If it hadn't been for the excellence of Angela's reading, she would have had no doubt about the casting of the play.

Angela scooted down in her seat when Lydia finished. "Juliet's supposed to look innocent," she muttered and then grimaced. "I'm sorry. She can't help the way she's built any more than I can."

She scooted even lower as the boys read. When they had finished and it was apparent that only one of them, Tommy Tucker, nicknamed appropriately "Little" Tommy Tucker, was capable of carrying the part of Romeo, Angela rubbed at her forehead and turned to Victoria. "That's it, then," she said bleakly.

"Okay," Joan called from the stage. "Thank you all for coming. I'll have the cast posted first thing Monday morning." At a collective groan from the students, Joan shook her head and laughed. "You think this is easy?" she asked.

Victoria and Angela stood up and silently began making their way up the aisle opposite the one where most of the kids congregated speculating on the outcome of the readings. Victoria remained silent. She could offer hope, but she knew it would probably be a false one, and she sensed that Angela wouldn't want that from her.

"Angela!" Joan Bailey's voice stopped them at the auditorium doors. Victoria saw the flash of expectation in Angela's eyes quickly masked as they turned to wait for the drama teacher who hurried up the aisle toward them.

Joan stopped in front of them, slightly breathless and looking as though she didn't know what to say. She reached out toward Angela but didn't touch her, closed her eyes briefly, and took a deep breath. "You know I can't give you the part, don't you?"

Angela nodded.

"You also know that you deserve it." Joan sighed. "If there was any way I could cast you as Juliet without jeopardizing the whole play, I would."

"I know, Mrs. Bailey," Angela told her, looking at Victoria, looking toward the door, obviously not wanting to have this conversation.

"I want to work with you," Joan went on. "And there's the senior play coming up."

Angela smiled wryly. "Tommy's not going to get much taller this year."

Joan's shoulders sagged. "No. Look," she said, "I know this isn't the reason you came, and if you think I'm way out of line, just tell me. The girls in my classes talk about your clothes, that you make them, and that you design them. I really need help with wardrobe. Would you—would you consider..."

"Can I think about it?" Angela asked.

They finally escaped. Victoria could feel Angela's disappointment as they walked together toward the parking lot, but the girl didn't voice it. They had just stepped off the curb when they heard the squeal of tires and a battered blue pickup came barreling out of the drive, forcing them to jump back.

"Wasn't that Will Hastings?" Victoria asked, catching her breath and staring after the truck.

Angela nodded. "Now there's someone who really has problems." She turned to Victoria and smiled. "We gave it our best shot, didn't we?"

"Yes."

Angela extended her hand. "Thank you."

Victoria smiled and took the girl's hand. "Thank *you*.

Angela hadn't completely shaken her dejected mood, but she was coming out of it. "No, I mean it," she said. "I appreciate your taking time you didn't have, and helping someone who isn't even one of your students and lending me the books and records. I want to do something for you.''

''That isn't—''

''Yes, it is,'' Angela interrupted. She grinned. ''My birthday is next week. The family is giving me a birthday party at the country club. Sort of a 'rite of passage' into adulthood. It's supposed to be a secret. I'd really like for you to come.''

Victoria felt the soft spring breeze suddenly become chill. A party. A family gathering at the country club with Phil there. She captured her wayward desires and pushed them back into reality, where they belonged. She didn't need to see him again; he wouldn't want to see her.

''No, really. But thanks.'' Escape. That was the only thing, rational or otherwise, that she could think of. She saw Angela gathering arguments to attempt to persuade her. Hastily she glanced at her watch. ''Just look at the time,'' she said lamely. ''I have to run.'' She shifted her armload of books and tried not to look guilty. ''I really do.''

Chapter Five

"Da-ad!"

Phil dug his forehead with the splayed fingers of one hand and shook his head slowly. Maybe this was the wrong time to suddenly become adamant, he knew she was still disappointed over losing the part in the play, but if this was a bad moment, when would the right one ever come? "No, Angela. Absolutely not. I'm glad you like this woman. I'm grateful to her for helping you. But I am not asking anyone else out because you want to find me a wife. Besides," he added, relaxing into a gentle teasing, "you've already told me she isn't my type."

"She isn't." Angela replaced the lid on the skillet of frying chicken and turned with regal dignity. "I'm *not* matchmaking."

Phil watched her warily, not trusting her at all when she slipped into her adult mode. "Then what...."

"I simply want to do something nice for someone who did something nice for me. You can understand that, can't you? After all, you're the one who raised me to be this way."

Phil silently conceded her that point and waited for her to continue.

"I think where I messed up was telling her that it was a surprise birthday party. She must have thought that if I wasn't supposed to know about it, I shouldn't be inviting someone to it. So if you asked her..."

"You know about the party?"

"Of *course* I know about the party. Ellie told me—"

Ellie. His cousin David's daughter. So much for keeping secrets in the family.

"She's a super lady, Dad. And it wouldn't be like it's a date. Just you letting her know it's all right for her to be there. I don't think she goes out much. You know, we hear things at school. Her dad's not real well so he can't help her with the ranch as much as he used to. One day Vickie was late coming in from chores—"

Vickie? Victoria was teaching freshman and sophomore grammar. Not literature. Not drama. Was this the mysterious teacher who was "not his type?"

"And Mr. Tankersley and I had the neatest talk. Do you know he used to be a federal marshall on border patrol? And that he used to ranch thousands of acres in New Mexico?"

Phil found his voice. "Vickie?"

Angela blushed. "Well, I don't call her that at school. But that's what her dad calls her, and I just kind of fell into the habit of thinking of her that way."

Victoria. The one woman he wanted to ask out, and he had chosen this moment to take a stand against his daughter's schemes. Would she come to the party if he asked her? And would it be only for Angela's sake if she came?

Sensing a softening in his resistance, Angela shed her pretense of being an adult. "Will you ask her? Please? I really do want her there."

Phil sighed. "I'll ask her, Angela. But as to whether she'll accept—I can't make any promises."

VICTORIA WAS IN THE CORRAL, hunkered down, replacing the drain stop to the horse trough she'd just finished scrubbing clean of its winter accumulation of algae and other assorted crud. She looked up, and Phil was there, leaning against the open gate and studying her silently, looking as he had in countless dreams and thoughts since she had sent him away last November. She blinked once, but he didn't disappear.

He pushed his hat back on his head and smiled, showing a flash of white teeth and an appealingly tilted mouth through his red beard. "Need some help?" he asked.

He might look as he had in her dreams, but she sure didn't. She was wet and dirty, with her hair straggling every which way out of its serviceable knot. "No," she said, fumbling with the shut-off valve and adjusting the automatic float to fill the tank. *Why was he here?*

"This isn't a good time," he said. "The problem is, I didn't know when would be a good time. Can we talk?"

Victoria stood awkwardly. Her hands were wet. She wiped them ineffectually against her water-splotched jeans. *Talk about what?* "Sure."

His eyes were busy, taking in every detail of her bedraggled appearance, and Victoria wanted to slink behind the tank. "Inside, maybe?" he asked. "So you won't get chilled."

For a person whose chosen career was peddling the English language, she wasn't doing very well; her command of that language had capriciously deserted her. She swallowed once and shrugged her shoulders. "Sure."

He followed her into the house and seated himself at the table while she turned the flame on under the waiting coffeepot, washed and dried her hands at the kitchen sink and rebuttoned the cuffs of her shirt.

She poured two cups of coffee and carried them to the table. "So," she asked as nonchalantly as she could, seating herself opposite him, "what do you want to talk about?"

"Partly," he said, "partly about Angela."

"Oh." Victoria took a sip of the steaming coffee, hiding her unreasonable disappointment. So this was a thank you call. She set the cup down and straightened in her chair. "She's a talented young woman."

"So I'm finding out. She appreciates the help you gave her, and—and so do I. Even though she didn't get the part."

"She should have gotten that part," Victoria said. "She knows it, I know it—and Joan Bailey knows it. Angela knew going in that she might not be cast as Juliet, but that didn't stop her from striving for excellence. You should be proud of her."

"I am." He, too, set his cup down, hesitating, but not taking his eyes from hers. "She wants you to come to her birthday party."

With one hand Victoria raked her hair, pushing the straggling tendrils away from her face while trying to think of a tactful refusal. "Phil, I—"

"It's her way of attempting to repay a kindness. You understand that, don't you?"

"Yes, I do. But I didn't expect anything in return except—" Except what? Except the possibility of seeing him again? Had that entered into her decision?

No. She'd already resolved that question; she didn't have to do it again. "Except the pleasure of working with someone as talented as she is."

"I know that."

"I certainly didn't use your daughter with the idea of some sort of future repayment."

"I know that."

She glanced up, surprised at his sharp tone.

"And I'm not going to use her, either," he said. "I told you the reason I was here was partly because of Angela. I'm finished talking about that part. I've delivered her message. I want to get on with the rest of it." His voice softened; his mouth tilted in a whimsical smile. "I want you to come to the party, too."

Victoria felt herself blanch, felt the chill of her flesh beneath damp clothes in spite of the warmth of the kitchen. She closed her eyes briefly. "Why?" she asked in a low voice.

"For the same reason I've had to fight with myself every day since last November to keep from picking up the telephone and calling you. I want to get to know you better. I want us to start over."

Victoria moved her head slowly from side to side, not in denial, but in stunned surprise at his words, at the chance she thought she had forever ruined.

"You didn't have time for me. I know that now. If I'd been half as alert as I pride myself on being, I'd have known it then. I'm not asking anything of you, Victoria, except the chance we never gave ourselves. Unless—unless you just can't stand the sight of me."

Victoria raised her hands to her face, cradling it, while she felt her pulse racing. "No," she said softly. She saw his hand on the table, knuckles whitened as he clutched his coffee cup. Surprising herself, she reached over and covered his hand with hers. "No," she repeated, "that's not the case at all. A chance?" she asked. It was more than she had let herself dream. "I'd like that, too."

VICTORIA SURVEYED herself critically in the mirror. Choosing something to wear had never before seemed such a difficult decision, or her ten-year-old wardrobe so woefully inadequate. Classic clothes remained in style; she'd prided herself on her choices when she had previously dug into the little-used back of her closet and even more recently when she had nipped in waistlines and adjusted hems for her new role as teacher. She'd been a fool to let Phil talk her into this. She laughed bitterly as she discarded still another dress and pulled a blue silk from its hanger. He hadn't talked her into anything. She'd jumped at the opportunity to be with him. Like a grateful puppy. But he wasn't here now, and her doubts were flying willy-nilly through her head, ricocheting off first one insecurity and then another.

"Vickie?" She heard her father call from the living room.

Hurriedly she pulled the blue silk over her head. "Be there in a minute, Pop," she called back. She smoothed the dress into place, stood back, and looked into the mirror again. For a moment she glimpsed the innocent, dream-filled girl she had been when the dress was new. Then she caught sight of the short, neatly filed nails that were all her work allowed her, the healing scratch along the back of her left hand, and the faint, ever-present calluses on the pads of her palms and fingers. She gave the dress one final adjustment and fled from her room and the image of herself in the mirror.

Just back from his weekly doctor's appointment, her father still wore his town clothes. He stood near the fireplace, studying the framed collection of family photographs that hung over the mantel, but he turned when she entered the room. Always bent over these days, he seemed to straighten when he looked at her, and the expression in his eyes softened. "You look beautiful."

Victoria hesitated just inside the room, embarrassed by the admiration she saw in his eyes. "Well," she said, gesturing awkwardly toward the softly clinging skirt, "I feel like a fraud. Or a hypocrite."

"Why?" Zack asked.

"You know, Pop," she began and then realized she couldn't tell him just how far her thoughts had taken her. "This isn't—this isn't me."

"It isn't?" He studied her across the distance of the room. "You look so much like your mother. Sometimes I forget." He turned to look at the pictures that spanned so much of his life. "Why, Vickie—and how—do we let ourselves forget what's really important to us?"

Victoria felt his unexpected sadness wash over her. She hurried across the room, surprising both of them with the fierceness of her embrace as she hugged him. "I love you, Pop."

WHEN PHIL ARRIVED, his expression was as appreciative as Zack's had been, and Victoria let herself relax. But in his car, on their way to the country club, her doubts returned. What was the matter with her? She had run the gauntlet of faculty teas, sorority rush and the inspection of Brad and Leah's parents, had come back to Pitchlyn County with her head held high after the foreclosure, knowing that neither she nor her father had been guilty of anything other than temporary poor judgment and an abundance of self-assuredness. She'd been exposed to class consciousness in the past but had thought herself above that kind of narrow thinking. But apparently she wasn't. Not much had been said to her face or in her presence since she had come back, but she had overheard one woman, a vicious gossip Victoria had always ignored, dissecting her at the grocery store. "It's about time that uppity Victoria Tankersley got taken down a peg or two." Now, nine years later, that scrap of conversation took on new, unwanted importance.

"You look beautiful," Phil said. He lifted his hand from the steering wheel and covered both of hers, which were clamped around the gift-wrapped book she held in her lap.

Startled by his unexpected words, his unexpected touch, she glanced up at him to see him smiling at her, his gray eyes still showing admiration. She returned his smile as his warmth spread from their joined hands, enveloping her, caressing her from that one point of contact.

THERE WAS NO QUESTION that the party at the small, newly constructed country club on the outskirts of Hillsboro was a gathering of the Wilcox clan. Victoria had never seen so much red hair, or so many tall, confident people in one place in her life. For the first several minutes, the only people she didn't have to look up to when she met them were the young children.

"You came!" Angela cried, pushing through the crowd. "I'm so glad."

"I am, too," Victoria told her, which wasn't altogether untruthful. "Thank you for inviting me." She held out the package. "And happy birthday."

"See, Dad, I told you she'd like the party." Angela took the package. "Thank you. I'll put this with the others," she said. "There's a ritual we have to go through after a while."

"Wanted me here, did she?" Victoria asked, but her tone was soft and indulgent as she watched Angela vanish into the crowd with an animated group of young people.

Phil chuckled. "Her life and future happiness depended on it." He draped his arm over Victoria's shoulder, started to remove it then apparently changed his mind. "Mine, too, I think," he said, giving her shoulder a gentle squeeze.

Before Victoria could respond to that cryptic comment, before she could even begin to sort through the questions it sent skimming through her, she heard a deep voice that sounded somewhere above her head. "Is this the Victoria Tankersley of unlimited patience and untold perception?" Victoria looked up to see a couple who had emerged from the crowd.

"My brother Ben," Phil told her, "and his wife Susan."

Susan was a tall brunette with a friendly, welcoming smile. Ben was a clean-shaven, less flamboyant version of Phil. And the district judge.

"Your Honor," Victoria said.

"Ben, please." He clasped her hand in a warm greeting.

"Oh, Lord, yes," Susan said, laughing. "He has a problem with his hat size already. It's up to the family to keep puncturing that ego of his before it gets completely out of hand."

"Hello."

Another member of the clan had joined the small, newly formed crowd.

"My little sister, Eunice," Phil told her.

His "little" sister was Eunice Wilcox Johnson, as tall as Angela, and the owner of the largest hardware and builders' supply company in the county.

"Thanks for what you did for Angela," Eunice said, extending her hand. Victoria took it and found the woman to have a surprisingly firm grip. "It was my pleasure," Victoria said.

Eunice grinned and looked at her appraisingly. "We've needed you at this school for a long time." Her grin twisted ruefully. "And I'm going to repay your kindness by imposing on you. I need to talk to you, Phil. And you, too, Ben."

Victoria felt the slight tension that tightened Phil's arm on hers, but he said nothing.

Eunice shook her head. "For once it's not a crisis involving me or mine. It's something the boys told me, and I need to know what to do with it."

After apologizing, Phil, Ben and Eunice walked to a deserted corner of the room, leaving Victoria with Susan. "I feel as though I ought to apologize to you, too," Susan told her, "for the fact that you've been abandoned to a roomful of strangers, but I'm afraid this isn't going to be the only time Phil gets dragged away from you today. How long have you been here? Ten minutes?"

"About that," Victoria said, puzzled.

"I think that might be a new record," Susan said. "There's a buffet table over here somewhere, and I'm starved. You want to help me find the food?"

Victoria looked across the room to where Phil stood engrossed in conversation with his brother and sister, then back at Susan. Whatever she had expected from the afternoon, this warm, obviously close-knit family had figured in it only peripherally, if at all. She turned to Susan, sensing in this woman, as in the rest of Phil's family, an open, nonjudgmental welcome. For Angela's friend? For Phil's date? Or maybe, just maybe, for herself, she let herself think. Susan took her silence as acceptance, linked her arm with hers and began leading her through the crowd.

There certainly was food, and in an amount suitable for the crowd, Victoria discovered when they reached the long tables laden with fresh vegetables, hot and cold hors d'oeuvres, dips and sauces. "Be sure to leave room for dinner," Susan warned her as they made their way down the tables, filling delicate china plates.

They found a relatively quiet corner, near the stone fireplace at one end of the room, but after the third person had approached them, wanting to meet Victoria and thank her for helping Angela, then wandering back into the shifting mass of people, Victoria shook her head. "Does everyone here know about that?"

"Probably," Susan told her. "We're pretty close."

A loud crash and the sound of breaking glass came from behind the double doors leading to the kitchen. "Oh, Lord," Susan said, instantly alert. "Please don't let that be dinner." She smiled apologetically at Victoria. "Will you excuse me? I've got to check. I'll be back in just a minute," she said over her shoulder as she started toward the kitchen. "I hope."

"They can be rather intimidating, can't they?"

For once the words weren't spoken at a level somewhere over her head. Victoria turned and found a petite woman a couple of inches shorter than she standing near her.

"Hi," the woman said. "I'm Leslie Nichols, David's wife." She nodded in the general direction of a group of men. "He's the only other non-giant in the room."

Victoria followed Leslie's fond glance to a dark-haired, slender man. David Nichols. He might be a non-giant physically, she thought, but that was the only way. The richest man in the county, maybe even in that part of the state, his holdings included ranches, petroleum, timber and race horses.

"When I first met David's family, I felt like a midget, and I went around with a permanent crick in my neck."

Having felt much the same way that afternoon, Victoria chuckled. "How did you ever sort them out?"

"Oh, it isn't that difficult," Leslie told her. "If you have a chance to meet them one at a time and recognize their special character traits. Ben is the calm voice of reason," she said. "Eunice is fiercely protective. And Phil, being the oldest, more or less 'fathers' everybody. I'm not sure it's fair to him, but I don't know what I would have done without him, and most of us feel the same way."

Leslie grinned. "The kids are a little harder to sort out." From where they stood they could see the deck and the young people who had gravitated to it, away from the adults. "The towheaded boy and the girl with the long, dark braid are our two, Mike and Ellie. The boy with Mike is young Ben. The twins—they're a year younger than Angela—are Eunice's. She has two more boys here somewhere. The quiet little girl by the pool is Brenda. She belongs—and you're every bit as confused as you were before I started this, aren't you?"

Victoria joined Leslie in quiet, conspiratorial laughter, enjoying the surprising sense of camaraderie she felt with the soft-spoken, unquestionably feminine woman who seemed as different from Phil's family as she herself did.

She glimpsed Phil across the room. He had left the corner and his conversation with Ben and Eunice wearing a frown of concentration, only to be stopped a few feet later by someone else, and again by still another person. Now he searched the crowd. Spotting her, he smiled and made his way to her side.

Leslie turned, sliding her arms around Phil's waist, and he enveloped her in a loose, comforting hug. "How are you doing?" he asked her.

"Fine." She smiled up at him. "The only way I could be doing any better is if I can pry David away from his talk about cows and cross-breeding." She stepped away from him. "But it's about time you got back to Victoria. I think she's getting ready to go into overload with a surfeit of our family."

"I'm sorry," Phil said when Leslie left them alone by the fireplace. "I didn't mean to throw you to the wolves, as nice as they are and as much as I love them."

"That's all right," she told him. "I didn't feel neglected at all. Susan and Leslie took care of me."

"Good," he said, leaning closer and speaking softly. "Now it's my turn."

SHE MIGHT NOT have felt neglected earlier, Phil thought as the afternoon turned to evening, but that was changing. Bringing her to the party hadn't been a mistake, he told himself, but thrusting her into the midst of his family before the two of them had had any time to themselves first, definitely had been. He was used to his family, accustomed to their seeking his advice, bringing him their problems for his input, sharing their triumphs. But was there more of it now? Because it seemed that every time he thought he was going to have a moment alone with Victoria, someone else materialized at their side.

Even at dinner, in the dining room that had been set up with small, linen-covered, candle-lighted tables in honor of Angela's first adult dinner party, there was no surcease. Wilma and John were their partners at the table set for four, and John wanted to talk about the advisability of switching to Santa Gertrudis cattle and his plans for pasture improvement. Unable to sidestep that conversation, Phil had drawn Victoria into it, inviting her to share her knowledge, but he had felt her slipping away from him and had known with a sickening wrench that she was wondering why she was there, why he had said he wanted her there when everyone and everything else seemed to be taking precedence over his avowed desire for them to get to know each other better.

Gratefully Phil heard the band hired for the evening tuning up in the lounge upstairs. He pushed back from the table and waited for John to come to a stop in what had become a monologue. "I've got to check on the musicians," Phil said. "Will you excuse me?" He turned to Victoria. "Come with me?" he asked and didn't imagine the relief he saw in her eyes.

Upstairs there wasn't much to do. The band had been recommended, and Phil had hired them primarily for the benefit of Angela and the other young people. He had previously discussed musical preferences with the leader of the group, a wiry young man who had obviously laundered his jeans and shampooed his long hair in honor of the country club setting. He had been pleased with his selection of a band, pleased with the general tone of the music they had settled upon. Now, with Victoria standing by his side in that clinging blue concoction she had surprised him by wearing, looking softly feminine, alluringly beckoning, he fought the urge to completely change the program. But of course, he couldn't do that, not tonight. He shook hands with the leader and welcomed the members of the group. "Just don't forget the old folks," he said.

"Don't worry, Mr. Wilcox," the young man said, laughing. "We know who signs the check."

Alone with her at last, Phil turned to Victoria in the dim room, seeing the glow of the soft lights in her eyes, the hint of a dazed, troubled smile on her small face, and realized that he had no idea of what to say to her. As the band began playing a waltz, he heard the noises of the rest of the party coming upstairs and saw John striding toward him, hand upraised as though ready to make still another point. He knew that he didn't want anyone else intruding on his time with her. "Dance with me," he said and, not waiting for her response, led her onto the floor.

She was light in his arms, small, fragile, and after her first start of surprise she relaxed in his embrace.

He had wondered how it would feel to hold her again. Wondered. Imagined. Asked himself countless times if it could possibly feel as right as the one time he had held her before. It did. With his daughter present, surrounded by his family, he felt the ache of wanting Victoria.

He sighed and held her closer. "I've wanted to do this all day," he admitted.

"You have?" she asked, sounding genuinely surprised. "Phil, I—"

He resisted the impulse to kiss her into silence. "Let's not talk," he said. "Not now. I've talked until I'm sick of the sound of my own voice. Let's just—" What? What could he say to her that wouldn't send her even farther away from him? Just let me hold you? Hardly. Not after having let everything else come between them that day. "Let's just dance."

She nodded, sighed and stepped closer to him, resting her cheek on his chest. He felt the soft thrust of her breasts against him, the brush of her thighs as they moved in the steps of the dance, the slide of silk beneath his hands across her back, and the ache grew.

They had two dances together before the band switched modes, catering to the young people. He saw the dazed expression in Victoria's eyes as she pulled away from him.

"There you are," John said, approaching him from across the room. Phil hid his groan and tightened his arm around Victoria's waist.

"Not now, John," Wilma said, intercepting her husband. She glanced at Phil and shrugged but showed more perception than her husband. "Give the man a break. You've been talking about those im-

provements for three months, and you can't do a
blasted thing about them tomorrow. I want to dance.''

"Are you crazy," John asked. "I can't do...
whatever it is you're supposed to do to that music.''

"Sure you can," Wilma said, winking at Phil as she
grabbed her husband's arm and dragged him onto the
dance floor.

Phil looked down at Victoria. There wasn't a chance
in hell they'd have any uninterrupted time if they
stayed until the end of the party. And if they stayed
several more hours, he was pretty sure he wouldn't
have a chance in hell with her at all. "Let's get out of
here," he said.

"Oh, can we?"

He tried not to smile at the relief in her voice. Instead, he took her arm and began leading her across
the room. "As soon as we say good night to the birthday girl.''

HE DIDN'T WANT to take her home. After spending
most of the day with her, he felt as though he hadn't
spent any time with her at all. And he didn't want their
one day together to be their last, to end as most of it
had seemed, with the two of them as far apart as ever.

He couldn't take her home. Not yet. He'd headed
south when they left the party, into the mountains. A
full moon silhouetted the distant peaks, bathed the
valleys in a silver glow, and cast shadows of the pines
and hardwoods across the road. Phil felt like an adolescent again, with a pretty girl in his car and no place
to take her, no place where they could have any privacy. And like an adolescent he wanted to pull to the
side of the road and take her into his arms. But he

couldn't do that, either. He barely understood his reasons for wanting to do so—physical desire, yes, but more than that; a need to hold her, to protect her, to keep the pressures of the world away from her if only for a little while; and for her to want him to do just that—and he was sure she wouldn't understand.

They had opened the car windows to let in the night sounds and gentle breeze. Now he saw her shiver, reminding him that in spite of Eunice's harbingers, true spring was at least a month away. He adjusted the heater and touched the buttons on the console that silently raised the windows. "Coffee?" he asked.

She smiled at him, and he saw in her the same hesitancy he felt. "Yes, I'd like that."

She faced him, one eyebrow raised and an unspoken question on her lips, when he turned into his driveway.

"Nothing is open this late except the all-night places," he said, feeling unreasonably defensive. "And they'll be full of the bar crowd and my clients."

When he parked in front of the garage, he saw her studying the neat cluster of well-lighted barns and metal corrals in the distance. And he watched her as they approached the house with its wide porch, hanging swing and flower beds and walked up the steps. Inside, he tried to see the house as it would appear to Victoria—the spacious rooms, the large, comfortable furniture, the colorful afghans and throw pillows, even the arrangement of silk flowers on the table behind the sofa.

"Very nice," she said quietly.

"Yes. Well..." He let out a deep breath, not liking the feeling of being tongue-tied and awkward but unable to break free of it. "The women in the family do their best to keep me domesticated." He gestured toward the living room. "Make yourself comfortable. It won't take but a minute to get the coffee started."

She looked at the living room then back at him, acting strangely subdued. "Why don't I come with you?"

He held the swinging door open for her and flipped the light switch on. The overhead fluorescents glowed to life, illuminating the neat white counters with everything in its place—thanks to Angela, he thought.

While he busied himself with filling the coffeepot and plugging it in, Victoria leaned against a counter, still subdued, and quietly studied the room. With nothing else to occupy his hands or his thoughts, he turned toward her. She was so small, so close, so *right* in his home and in his life. Unable to help himself, he raised his hand to her face. "Victoria, I . . ."

She looked up at him, bending her head back to meet his eyes, and he had never before been so aware of his size. He felt like a big red bear looming over Victoria. Without stopping to think, he shifted his hands to her waist, lifting her and seating her on the countertop.

He saw the surprise in her eyes replaced with a soft expectancy. Her breathing was shallow; her lips slightly parted.

"I didn't mean to do this," he said, touching her face, running the tips of his fingers into her hair, lowering his mouth to hers.

Her lips were soft, softer even than he had remembered, welcoming him, moving beneath his in gentle response. He took that response, glorying in it, urging it onward with a need that shook him, until, sighing, he pulled away from her. It was either that or take them farther than either of them was prepared to go so soon.

He leaned his forehead against hers. "I didn't bring you here as an excuse to make love to you."

She lifted her hands to his cheek, caressing beard and cheek with her fingertips. "I know that, Phil."

For a moment, he allowed himself the painful enjoyment of her innocently erotic touch. Then he pulled away from that, too, and looked at her. Her eyes were troubled but still filled with expectancy; her breathing was deeper now, but her lips were still parted. While he watched, her eyes darkened. Her hand slid from his cheek to the back of his head, and she leaned forward.

Need fueled need as he again claimed her mouth. Her arms were around him, holding him, one hand at the back of his neck, the other clutching his shoulder, as his were around her, needing her closer than humanly possible as his hands sought and found the varying textures of silk: silken fabric, silken hair, silken flesh.

"Dad? Are you in there?" He heard Angela's voice as the swinging door flew open, bouncing against the doorstop. He turned his head abruptly to see his daughter standing in the doorway, eyes wide, mouth open, and Maxine peering around her, looking equally astounded.

"Oops," Angela said. "I—uh—Stacy spilled coke on me...I came home to change clothes. I'm sorry, I'll get out of here."

Phil felt his shoulders sag. He couldn't look at Victoria. Not yet. He had a pretty good idea of how much this had embarrassed her, and he was too afraid of what he would see. He stepped away from her and listened to the girls' footsteps echoing down the hall-way, to his daughter's voice. "Not one word, Maxine. If I hear anything about this at school, anything at all, I'll never design another outfit for you as long as I live. Do you understand?"

He heard the soft thud of Victoria easing herself from the cabinet top. Knowing he could put it off no longer, he turned toward her. She was busy adjusting her clothes, busy looking anywhere but at him.

"I—I think I'll pass on the coffee, Phil," she said too brightly. "Would you mind taking me home now?"

"No. No, I . . ." What could he say. She'd heard what he'd heard. And he couldn't be mistaken: she'd felt what he'd felt.

He stopped her in her march toward the kitchen door. Catching her arm, he turned her, forcing her to look up at him. He saw the pain of embarrassment in her eyes and hated himself for having put it there, but there was no way he was letting it end like this.

"We have to see each other again."

Victoria closed her eyes briefly, then met his. She swallowed once. "Yes," she said, with what sounded to him much like defeat in her voice. "Yes, I know."

Chapter Six

Victoria sat at the kitchen table, account books and checkbook in front of her, an old electric calculator to one side, surrounded by stacks of bills in varying degrees of neatness and with a good two yards of adding machine tape curling from the top of it and dangling down to the floor. Sunday afternoon was the only day she had enough uninterrupted time to tackle the mess of their accounts.

She felt the acid roiling in her stomach and knew that postponing what she had to do would only make matters worse. Not that matters could be much worse. And it wasn't the unending stream of bills in front of her that brought that thought to her mind.

She leaned back in her chair, closing her eyes against the memories of the previous night. Against the sight of Angela and Maxine standing open-mouthed and wide-eyed in Phil's kitchen door. She needed the job at Hillsboro High School that she had been all but promised for the next year, after she finally had her degree. Needed the paycheck. And if she hadn't completely destroyed her chances of getting the job, she had destroyed any effectiveness she might have as a teacher if word got out about her perched on Phil

Wilcox's kitchen counter in reckless abandon of what most of the parents in this community considered proper moral behavior.

And for what? For a few minutes in his arms? For a few minutes of forgetting the differences between the two of them? For a few minutes of forgetting bills and problems and responsibilities? For a few minutes of feeling alive and wanted, as a woman, for the first time in years, maybe ever?

All right. So the man was ninety-eight percent wonderful, attractive and sexy and caring. So everyone in that horde of people he called a family loved and respected him. So he had the innate ability to inspire their trust, help them shoulder their responsibilities. At least they had something to give him in return. What did she have? Time to spend with him? Provided he even wanted her to after he reconsidered their day together? Hardly. Not without stealing it from something that needed doing. No. The only thing she really had in abundance was spread out on the table in front of her. She picked up the nearest stack of bills and dropped them, one at a time, to the table: hardware company, feed store, veterinarian supplies, hospital bills . . . She let the remaining stack slither to the table.

And now this latest problem: how to find enough hay to finish out the remainder of the feeding season. And how to pay for it if she did find it, because most of her neighbors had been caught with as short a supply as she had, and any she found would come at a premium price.

She let herself think of Phil's place as it had looked in the moonlight. Perfect pastures. Perfect corrals. Perfect barns. Perfect registered Santa Gertrudis cattle. She might have known, without spending a day with his family, that even his cattle would be red. She rubbed at her forehead, banishing her ungracious thoughts and recognizing them for the defensive measure they were. Because she knew that, given an opportunity and in spite of the discomfort she had at times felt, she would repeat the day she had spent with Phil. Because she knew that she wanted nothing more than to be back in his arms, feeling the solid strength of him enveloping her, feeling the magic that had seemed to flow between them, feeling delicate and protected and wanted.

She heard the sound of Pop's truck pulling into its parking space, straightened in her chair, and grabbed for a stack of invoices and her discarded pencil. Zack entered the kitchen, bringing a rush of cool air with him, and walked directly to the coffeepot. She studied him carefully while he poured a cup of coffee. His regular afternoon tour of the ranch had been good for him. There was color in his cheeks from the fresh air; a sparkle in his eyes from feeling he was at least doing something to help in the management of the ranch.

He carried his coffee to the table and seated himself in his chair, glancing at the organized disarray on the table. "How are we doing?"

"We'll make it," she told him. She grinned. "Of course, the new calf crop will determine how *well* we make it."

"That red shorthorn dropped her calf this morning."

Victoria's grin softened to a smile. Without a strictly scheduled breeding program, they could expect their calves any time from December into March, but a new birth was always an occasion of wonder for her. "How is it doing?"

"Fine," Zack said. "It was up and nursing."

The tone of his voice and his slight frown alarmed her. "Is something wrong?"

Pop shook his head. "It doesn't have the size her calves usually have." He sighed. "None of the calves off that new bull have."

Victoria felt the acid in her stomach churning again. That bull had been an expense they were still scrimping to make up for. "They still might take off and grow," she suggested. "We both know it's weaning weight that counts."

"They might." Pop looked dubious. He glanced at the account book. "But we'd better start figuring out how we're going to replace him, just in case."

"Pop...." She couldn't argue with him about replacing the bull. His word was law when it came to matters involving livestock. But there was something that needed to be said, and she had rehearsed countless times how she would approach him. Give him two alternatives, neither of them totally acceptable, but the one she knew he would reject first. "We need some operating capital."

Zack took a swallow of coffee and leaned back in his chair. "Doesn't everybody. Ted was telling me in his last letter that it's the same back home. He's doing better than some of his neighbors, but still, he's feeling the pinch, too."

Victoria shook her head. She wasn't callous to her Uncle Ted's problems, but she refused to let her father sidetrack her this time. "As I see it, we could sell that eighty acres across the creek."

She saw Zack's head beginning to move in denial.

"And we could use the money to improve the herd, equipment and facilities we have."

"That's the best hay meadow we've got."

"I know." She paused. "And cutting back won't really help in the long run." Say it, Victoria, she prompted herself. Get it out in the open. At least get him thinking about it. "I'll be working next fall. I can probably even find some kind of work this summer, after graduation. With a regular paycheck coming in, we wouldn't have any trouble repaying a loan. One big enough to help us out of the hole we're in now. Maybe even—maybe even pick up part of the Stevens's place to the north of us. It's for sale, all or part of it."

Zack's lips whitened. His jaw clenched in an all-too-familiar stubborn set. "No mortgages. You know how I feel about that. That's what got us in the mess we're in now. No. We pay as we go, or we don't go."

Victoria felt the pencil digging into her hand as she clenched it. Her father reached over and clasped her hand. "Vickie, honey, I know things are tough right now, but they're looking better. Remember nine years ago? Even five?"

Victoria gave a quick, abrupt nod.

"Next fall, you'll be teaching, doing what you've always wanted to do. And I'll be—I'll be better. Things have a way of working out. And God knows, both of us are ready for that to happen."

He released her hand and picked up his coffee cup, once again leaning back in his chair. "You haven't told me about the party." Victoria glanced up to see the remnants of a fleeting smile on Zack's face. "Did you and Wilcox have a good time?"

PHIL SPENT Sunday morning riding over his ranch on horseback. That was something he seldom did, something he rarely thought he had the time to do. And to be honest, he admitted to himself, it was something that wasn't often necessary. That morning it was necessary. Alone in the saddle was the only place he could ensure for himself the solitude to pursue his thoughts.

His spread was about the same size as Victoria's, but he knew that was probably the only similarity between the two places. He stood in the stirrups surveying rich, valley pasture, not the wild hill country she had to constantly fight to keep from reverting to the pinoak and blackjack forest it had once been. His fences stretched straight and true on metal posts, kept that way by a hired foreman and ranch hands; he suspected that Victoria and an occasional hired laborer saw to hers. And his cattle, sleek registered breeding stock, all heavy with calves they would soon begin dropping, brought a hell of a lot more in private sale than her beef cattle did on the open market.

He wondered how different his place would look, how different his life would be, if he hadn't had the money to invest in the well-tended acres that stretched around him, in the starter herd of registered stock, if he hadn't had the income from his law practice to feed into his ranch until it became self-sustaining. But he didn't really have to wonder. He knew he'd be in the same financial slavery as most of his neighbors were, as Victoria was, struggling to hold on to a way of life, struggling to hold on to what previous generations had built and nurtured. Struggling. Constantly battling the weather and disease and the vagaries of an undependable market.

He thought of Jim Thompson, a neighbor, a man he'd known since they entered grade school together. He'd guided Jim through bankruptcy proceedings that winter, unable to work out any restructuring agreement on his debts. Jim's father had taken a small family farm, converted it to ranching as farming steadily moved northward to the river bottom land, and made a moderate success of it. Jim had taken over when his father died, working himself and his wife into early middle age, expanding with the market, adding the equipment and structures that the growing operation demanded. Jim had been born in the ranch house; his mother, who lived with him, had known no other home for almost fifty years.

Now she did. Now Jim and his family, including his mother, lived in a small, rented, three-bedroom frame house on a fifty by one hundred foot lot in Fort Smith, Arkansas, while Jim, a man who had spent almost forty years outdoors, worked the all-night shift on an assembly line at a furniture factory. And Phil would never forget the bleakness in his friend's eyes after the last hearing, after Jim's life had been forever changed. "It's over," Jim told him. "Maybe I ought to be glad. At least I've been put out of my misery. I'm not still out there trying to hang on to a dream, like an old horse that's broken its leg. Still trying to get up. Still trying to plow. Knowing it's coming, but still trying to avoid that final, inevitable bullet."

Phil eased his horse, a big chestnut gelding, away from its intended destination of a meandering stream and grove of trees and headed back toward the house. Was that how Victoria felt? That she was waiting for the final bullet? She'd never let him know if it was. He knew that much about her.

What else did he know? She was resilient, but she wasn't nearly as tough as she thought she was. When had she drawn that protective armor around her? Some time in the last nine years, he knew. And what would it take to get through it? That, he didn't know. She wanted him; her response proved that much to him and also proved that she didn't want to want him. Phil didn't let himself examine too closely why this was important to him, he just accepted that it was. Examination could come later.

There ought to be something he could do to help her. There ought to be something she would *let* him do. Strangers on the street expected that from him. But he knew he would have to be careful. And he also knew that it would be dangerous for him to allow her too much time to dwell on the disastrous ending to the previous night before pressing the advantage she had given him with her grudging agreement to see him again. But how, he wondered as he urged his horse into a run. He couldn't just show up on her doorstep, the way he wanted to, with no plan in mind. *How?*

INADVERTENTLY, Angela provided Phil with a solution. She also provided him with a strong urge to permanently gag and muzzle his daughter. They spent a quiet Sunday afternoon together. Unnaturally quiet. So much so that the silence finally penetrated Phil's troubled thoughts and he became aware of the questioning and suspicious glances his daughter cast at him with an unnerving regularity.

"All right," he said as they stacked the dinner dishes into the dishwasher, half suspecting what she was trying not to say, and knowing he had to force this confrontation. "You might as well say it."

"Say what?" Angela mumbled as she closed and started the dishwasher.

"If I knew what," he said softly, "I wouldn't have to ask you. Come on," he prompted. "We don't keep secrets from each other."

"We don't?" She picked up a sponge and began scrubbing at the spotless counter, then tossed the sponge at the sink and whirled on him. "All right! It's about you and Vickie. Maxine won't say anything, I made sure of that. But, Dad! How could you?"

Phil closed his eyes briefly. He knew he had to proceed carefully, but he also knew this was something he had to make his daughter understand. "What do you think men and women do together, Angela? Do you believe that because we've passed the age of twenty-five we no longer feel physical attraction, or affection, or the need to share those feelings with another person? You're the one who's been urging me to get married again. You're the one who wants me to find someone I can care for. Didn't you carry that out to a logical conclusion?"

Angela's mouth opened, but no words came out. And then they came out in a rush. "You...you didn't do that with *all* those women?"

Phil rubbed his hand across his face, feeling the abrasion of his beard and the frustration of trying to communicate. He shook his head. "No. But I like Victoria. It's too soon to say what will happen between us, if anything does, but I really like her. And that shouldn't surprise you; you like her, too."

"Yeah, but.... Oh, Lord. Dad, I didn't think you... She's nothing like the list. I mean, she was *my* friend. And I—"

He watched as her face blanched, and he knew what she had stopped herself from saying. "And you talked to her, didn't you?"

Angela nodded silently.

"About me?"

"Some."

"About—" Realization dawned on him. "Oh, no. Dammit, Angela, I told you I didn't want you matchmaking in the first place, and I specifically told you I didn't want you talking about it."

"I know." She lifted her head defiantly. "And I didn't. Not to any of the kids. Because I knew they'd talk about it, too. But Vickie was different. Maybe she didn't hear," she offered. "It was Wednesday. We'd stopped work early so she could get ready for her class. She was awful busy. And she never said anything to me about it later."

Victoria had heard. Phil had no doubt about that. She'd probably also heard about the string of women he had been seen going out with. And to carry it one step further, as he knew he had to, she was probably in the process of convincing herself that she was just another of that string, which was one more problem they didn't need.

But it wasn't the only problem he had at the moment. He'd been accused of bellowing in the past, but seldom at his daughter, and seldom in anger. She looked so insecure. Child and woman. Both and neither. He wanted her to be aware of the consequences of her actions; he didn't want her intimidated. He took a step toward her and opened his arms. "Come here, squirt," he said.

She hesitated and then ran to him, letting him envelop her in a hug. "Don't worry," he told her. "It will all work out." And he hoped to God he was right.

VICTORIA HURRIED through her shower and into her last pair of clean jeans. Gathering up a load of laundry, she carried it through the kitchen and dumped it and detergent into the washing machine.

"I'll put those in the dryer when I get home tonight," she told Zack, still seated at the table with a cup of coffee and a magazine.

He nodded, apparently lost in the article he was reading, and Victoria looked around, searching for books and notebook to take with her. She found her notebook on top of the refrigerator, and when she lifted it down, the mail she had gathered from the box at the bottom of their hill fell to the floor.

"Forgot about that," she said idly, stooping to scoop up the mail. "There's a letter here from Uncle Ted," she told her father, handing it to him on top of the stack of junk mail. "What are you two up to, anyway?"

Zack looked slightly startled at the question, then cocked his head, listening. "There's a car coming."

Victoria grinned at his delaying tactics, wondering why he thought them necessary, but as she debated questioning him about them, she, too, heard a car groaning up the steep incline of their drive.

Puzzled, she flipped the switch for the yard light and went to stand in the door. She recognized Phil's Oldsmobile the moment it crested the hill. She felt her hands grow clammy and her throat dry simultaneously. She'd told him she'd see him again and then had spent the past four days trying to deny to herself that she had. She sagged against the doorway, knowing he couldn't see her yet. And his timing was perfect. She had all of five minutes before she had to leave.

He unfolded himself from his car and started around the front of it, and Victoria straightened in the doorway, conscious of the strength he exuded and the innate grace of his movements. She fixed a polite smile on her face. "Hello, Phil."

"Hello." He stopped at the bottom of the steps, searching her eyes and her face, and for once eye level with her. Then, as though remembering why he had come, he smiled. "I've got an appointment tonight. I wondered if I could persuade you to ride along with me."

For a moment Victoria considered how she could accept his invitation. She hadn't missed class all semester, in spite of the January ice. Why not, just for once, do what she wanted, say to hell with responsibilities and go off with him into the night? But she had a paper due that evening, and a short conference scheduled with her adviser after class. She felt her smile fading as slowly she began to shake her head.

"Good evening, Mr. Tankersley," Phil said, looking past her shoulder into the kitchen.

"'Evening, Wilcox."

"I'm sorry, Phil. I have a class tonight."

"In Durant?" he asked. "At the college?"

She resisted the impulse to cock an eyebrow at him and ask him just where else he thought she would have time for a class. "Yes."

"Great. That's where my appointment is. In Durant, not the college." He put his hand on her shoulder, turning her toward the house, as he vaulted up the steps. "Get your jacket. I hate making that drive by myself, especially at night."

She saw Zack leaning back in his chair, studying the two of them and obviously as suspicious of the coincidence as she was. She didn't care. She grabbed her jacket and books and let Phil hurry her out the door.

But she did wonder. And once they had left the drive and headed south into the mountains, her thoughts refused to let go of how remarkably convenient his appointment had turned out to be. Must be something about the luxurious interior of his car, she thought; every time she got in it, she found herself as tongue-tied, doubtful and insecure as a teenaged girl on her first date.

She couldn't ask him if he had manufactured a fictitious appointment in order to spend time with her. To her that sounded like the height of ego. "Who... who is your appointment with?"

"An unofficial resource," he told her. "Someone I consult occasionally when I need information and don't want any record of that information."

"Oh," she said, when he showed no indication of elaborating. "How... how was your week?"

She saw a flash of white through his beard as he smiled. "Cattle and clients. How was yours?"

"Cattle and kids." And that pretty much exhausted her supply of small talk.

He lifted one hand from the steering wheel and rested it on hers on the armrest between them. "I missed you."

She felt the warmth from their joined hands begin its insidious way up her arm, spreading through her, and relaxed against the seat. "I missed you, too," she admitted.

"You haven't had any problems, have you? At school."

She knew what he meant by problems: Maxine's wagging tongue about the spectacle she had witnessed Saturday night. She tensed and tried to move her hand, but he refused to release her. "No. No problems."

"Good." He let out a pent-up breath. "We're going to have to talk about that." He waited, but she gave him no encouragement, made no protest. "I'm sorry about the embarrassment it caused you," he told her. "If I had known the outcome, I might have done things differently, but I'm not sure I could have stopped what happened between us. I am sure that, except for the ending, I have no regrets about what happened."

"So," he said, releasing her hand when she made no response and once again gripping the steering wheel. "How is school?"

Regrets, she thought numbly. He had no regrets. Did she? Did she really?

"You are enjoying teaching, aren't you?"

She became aware of the length of time she had remained silent and of his uneasy efforts to break that silence. "Yes," she said. No. No regrets. Not a one. She smiled into the darkness. "Yes, I am. A lot more than I expected to, because it's so different from what I had planned to be doing. But in a special kind of way, what I'm doing is rewarding. And necessary."

She laughed softly. Once again his hand covered hers, encouraging her.

"We were having a segment on diagramming sentences yesterday," she told him. "One of those sessions that can be deadly dull to a fourteen-year-old, and the inevitable question came: 'Why do I have to learn this? What good is it going to do me when I'm going to be...' You can fill in the blank, because I'm sure there have to be almost as many endings to that as there are students to ask it. In this case, it was 'working cows the rest of my life.' I had to admit to that classroom of students that when I have a cow down in a squeeze chute and can't get her up, I sometimes lose my command of the English language. But it gave me an opportunity to tell them something very important, to share with them what I think is the true purpose of any school English program, and I think—I hope I reached at least some of them."

He squeezed her hand. "And why do I have to learn this, Miss Tankersley?" he asked in a gently teasing voice. "What good is it going to do me when I'm going to be a lawyer?"

She chuckled and turned her hand, lacing her fingers with his, and enjoying this moment of quiet sharing. "Do you want the soapbox edition or the edited version of my answer?"

"Either one, teacher."

Teacher. For the first time in years, she felt like one. "Why is it so hard for them to understand, Phil? The purpose of language is to aid in communication. And it doesn't matter what field they go into, or how well they know that field, if they can't communicate their knowledge, to co-workers, to businessmen, to bankers, even to the vet when they're trying to explain what's happened to the cow, they're going to be at a disadvantage. But if they can speak well, use the correct word, construct a sentence, or write a decent letter, unfair or not, most people are going to pay more attention to what they say and to what they appear to know."

THEIR EASY COMMUNICATION lasted throughout the drive and until Phil pulled into an on-campus visitor's parking space, confirmed the time and place of their later meeting, and watched Victoria's slender figure merge with other jeans-clad night students hurrying along the sidewalks and into the maze of buildings.

Phil stayed in the car for a moment, caught up in the sense of idealistic, purpose-filled activity that a college campus never failed to invoke in him and thinking about the drive, which had seemed much shorter than the clock on the dashboard proved it to have been.

He wondered if she was as aware as he of how rare, how special, that time had been. Phil made his living with oratory and argument; his days were filled with small talk and business communications. But he seldom revealed anything of himself, other than on a superficial level, to anyone outside his family. Tonight he had. With Victoria, he had found himself voicing the frustration he sometimes felt at being constantly on call to clients who thought nothing of picking up the telephone in the middle of the night, or Sunday dinner.

And Victoria? He wondered if she were aware of how much of herself she had revealed. The idealism she swore she no longer felt, the sensitivity she masked with her avowed pragmatism, the vulnerability buried beneath layers of competency. He didn't think so. He wasn't sure why she felt she had to deny those things, but he knew if she had known how much she was exposing the woman she truly was, she would have pulled back into her shell, hiding from him. Maybe even hiding from herself, Phil thought in a moment of insight.

She'd suspected he'd manufactured the story of an appointment in Durant. That much had been evident in the awkwardness that always seemed to surround their first moments together. He hadn't. His own in-grained sense of fair play wouldn't let him do that. And her own straightlaced honesty and stiff-necked pride would have rejected such a ploy on his part. But he had made the appointment for a necessary conver-sation, when a telephone call would probably have worked as well, because of her. And—he glanced again at the clock on the dashboard—if he didn't get a move on, he was going to be late.

Brad was already waiting at the restaurant when Phil arrived. He lifted an arm, signaling Phil to the back booth where he was seated, and Phil felt himself responding to the man's welcoming smile in spite of the subject of their upcoming talk. He had met Brad Hill when his friend was principal of Hillsboro's ju-nior high school. After two years in that position, Brad had finally admitted that school administration was not for him and had taken a job with Court Re-lated and Community Services, an organization deal-ing with troubled and delinquent juveniles. Along with the change in job had come a transfer, and although Brad did not live in Durant, he lived close enough so that Phil had not felt he was imposing on their friendship when he suggested the meeting.

He returned Brad's hearty handclasp and greeting and scooted into the opposite side of the booth, silent until the waitress filled his coffee cup and left.

"Okay, good buddy," Brad asked. "What brings you to God's country?"

"God's country?"

Brad laughed. "Close enough. If you think parts of Pitchlyn County are isolated, you should see the place Janie and I have now. Forty acres on a bluff twenty-five miles from the nearest town. It took us a year to get electricity in there, and three tries to get a decent well. But it was worth it. The view is better than anything Bierstadt or Moran ever dreamed of painting. And the silence—the silence will heal your soul. So? When are you coming for a visit?"

Phil chuckled. "When are you getting a helipad?"

Brad joined in his laughter. "Last winter I began to think we were going to need one. Seriously, though, Janie and I would love to have you down for a weekend. You can even bring one of those lovely ladies I've been hearing about. Impress her with how wholesome your friends are."

Phil leaned back in the booth and shot Brad a questioning glance.

"Hey, friend, we're isolated, but not *that* isolated. Word travels."

Phil grimaced. "And grows as it does. Believe me, the rumors of my exploits are vastly overrated."

"Shucks," Brad drawled. "Well, if you didn't come to swap locker room stories, and you knew I wouldn't have any to trade before you came...." Brad's voice lost its teasing tone. "What does bring you all this distance?"

Phil sighed, knowing he had put off doing anything about this for too long, in spite of the talk he and Ben had had earlier in the week. "A client. And a problem."

"It figures." Brad pushed his coffee cup to one side. "Do I take notes?"

"No," Phil said, shaking his head. "That's why I'm talking to you instead of the local agency."

"Okay. Off the record, it is. Spill it."

"The boy is a client of mine," Phil told him. "A juvenile. He's been in and out of trouble for years. He hasn't been adjudged delinquent, but he's headed that way."

"Do I know him?"

Phil nodded. "Yes, I hope you won't mind if I don't give you any names, just yet." He waited a moment, then, accepting Brad's silence as agreement, proceeded. "Last Saturday, Eunice told me and Ben something her boys had shared with her in confidence. They believe that the boy had been beaten by his father, and that it hadn't been the first time."

"Any evidence?" Brad prompted.

"No. He's always in fights. Bruises and cuts and scrapes are a way of life to him."

"Do you know the father?"

"Oh, yes. He's a hard worker, abrasive, drinks some, but to my knowledge he's never been in trouble for any alcohol-related offense. He seems genuinely disgusted by his son's behavior and puzzled about how any child of his could act the way he has."

"Which brings you back to the boy."

"Yeah." Phil noticed the waitress hovering nearby and nodded to her to refill their cups, once again waiting for her to leave before speaking. "I've hesitated about talking to him, because, to be quite honest, we don't have a good rapport. He's belligerent, and highly defensive behind all of his offensive actions."

"Things abuse could account for."

"I know," Phil said. "I don't want the boy hurt unnecessarily. But neither do I want his father hurt by an unfounded charge. That's why I haven't taken this to the local agency. And to be honest, I don't know if I can believe anything the boy tells me. Whether he would deny actual abuse in some sort of macho bravado or from a fear of incurring more, or whether he would admit to it falsely, using it as justification for his actions."

"You, my friend, are in a hell of a mess."

Phil smiled wryly. "Tell me about it."

"I could take it to the agency for you, anonymously," Brad offered. "That way you wouldn't be involved."

Phil shook his head. "I am already involved."

"You always are." Brad shifted in the booth and took a sip of his coffee. "Okay. I'm not sure I agree with your decision to keep silent but I certainly understand your reasons. You did come for advice, didn't you?"

Phil grinned at him. "Let's just say I knew I was going to get it whether I asked for it or not."

"Yeah. You are. Okay. Talk to the boy. Feel him out even if you don't just come straight out and ask him. He needs a confidant. I don't suppose Eunice's boys could—"

"No," Phil interrupted. "He doesn't run in their circle, and what they told Eunice was apparently learned by accident."

"Okay. Keep an eye on the boy. Keep an eye on the father. At the first indication you have that there may be any basis to the rumor, you take it to the agency. Don't try to do anything about it yourself. We have staff trained to discover the truth. And believe it or not, we can be discreet, when necessary.''

PHIL SEEMED QUIET and reflective when he picked her up, and for a while that was all right with Victoria. She had some reflecting to do herself, about the conference with her adviser, about Phil and her varied reactions to him. But soon she missed the companionship they had shared on the drive down.

She turned in the seat, facing him, and placed her hand on the armrest. "How did your appointment go?" she asked. "Did you get the information you needed?"

He shrugged. "I think I more or less just reinforced what I already knew."

"Will that be enough?"

"I don't know." He glanced at her, silent for a moment. "Victoria, do you have any contact at school with students who are not in your classes?"

"Some," she said. "Not much. Why?"

Again he was silent for a moment. "No reason." He covered her hand with his. "Never mind. How was your conference with your adviser?"

Now Victoria hesitated. "He dangled the carrot of a master's degree program in front of me," she said lightly. Thrust it in her face was a more apt description. Tempted her with the impossibility of advanced studies.

"Are you going to go for it?"

"I don't think so." She knew so. There was no way she could justify the time or expense. "I don't really need a master's for high school English," she said, "and I—" She looked away from him, out into the night, searching for some truthful, and final, way to close this subject. "I know I can't stand another two years or more of driving this road at night."

Phil took over the conversation, leading them into safer topics, reestablishing their earlier camaraderie. Until they turned off the highway onto the road that led to her home. Until she remembered that their evening was almost over. Until she remembered how disastrously each previous evening they had shared had ended.

Tonight's apparent closeness had to have been a fluke, she told herself, needing to believe that was so: a moment out of time, a memory she could treasure. She and Phil had nothing in common. Not really. She had tried not to let Angela's innocent confidences bother her, but now they did. She was so far removed from Phil's mythical "perfect" woman that the differences were almost laughable. Tall, blonde, educated and feminine. She could disregard the first two attributes, rationalize around the third, but the final one—no one who had spent time with her in a cattle pen could ever call her feminine. The problem was, with him, especially in his arms, she felt feminine.

"Watch out for the cattle guard," she warned him unnecessarily as he turned into their drive.

And Phil needed someone feminine. A counterpoint to his strength. Someone to continue the loving domestication the women of his family had begun. Someone on whom he could shower the protection he now seemed bent on giving everyone in the county. Someone to nurture and return the kind of love she now sensed he was capable of sharing. Someone who had something to give him in return.

She scrambled for her books as he turned into the parking space, had them clutched in her arm by the time he braked to a stop. "Thanks for the ride, Phil," she said quickly, reaching for the door handle. "I really enjoyed this evening."

"Victoria?"

He mustn't kiss her. Twice before he had; twice before she had not recognized herself in the woman who responded to him. The memory of this evening's closeness would never threaten her; another memory of another time lost in his arms would be intolerable. "It's late," she said, sliding out of the car and easing the door shut. "Thanks again."

Phil caught her by the arm before she reached her back steps, knowing that he should have let her go, knowing that there was no way he could have done so. Gently he tugged on her arm until she turned to face him. Then, with one large hand, he cupped her face, urging her to look up at him and feeling the tremor that ran through her. Then slowly, against his better judgment, almost against his will, he bent toward her. He heard her moan as his lips touched hers, heard the soft thud as her books hit the ground, felt her resistance crumble as her arms went around him. And then the kiss that had started as a gentle salute, a tender good-night for the closeness they had shared, took on a blazing life of its own, drawing the two of them into a vortex of pulsating need and frustrated longing.

Somehow he managed to regain control of himself, to reluctantly end the kiss, to hold her quietly against him while he tried to subdue his ragged breathing and his racing heart.

She pushed away from him and took an unsteady step backward. "Phil," she asked in a little voice. "What do you want from me?"

Want? When he had first met her again, he'd tried to convince himself that she in no way resembled the kind of woman he thought he wanted; now he knew that she was more than he'd ever hoped to find. He lifted his hand, once again cradling her face, and felt still another tremor run through her as he studied her eyes in the moonlight. He'd scare her away if he told her just how much he wanted from her; the thought scared even him.

"Would you believe," he asked shakily, "would you believe I'm just as confused by what's happening between us as you are?"

Chapter Seven

She didn't love Phil Wilcox. She couldn't. Victoria braked the pickup to a stop at the north end of number two pasture. In a year, maybe two, she could begin to think about a personal life, a future for herself, but not before then. And by then, Phil would have long since given up on her.

She eased herself from the cab of the truck, leaving the door open, and walked slowly toward the herd of cattle enjoying the March sun. Pop had checked them that morning, but with so many of the cows still calving, twice a day checks were not often enough. Tufts of green dotted the winter brown of the pasture. Victoria cast a suspicious glance at the clear, blue sky. She'd managed to find some hay. Maybe it would be enough. Maybe this year, nature would be kind for a change and spare them a March snow. Fat chance, she thought, kicking over an uprooted tuft of dried grass. There was an old saying that God wasn't a rancher, and sometimes when she watched herself, her father and her neighbors waging their on-going war with the predictably unpredictable weather, she almost believed it.

What *did* Phil want from her? She had asked herself that question countless times in the weeks since their drive to Durant. At first she thought it must have been sex; the attraction between them was so flammable, the tension between them thrumming with an intensity she had never felt before. But except for kisses that left her longing for more, and had to have been worse for him, there had been nothing else. He had given her no indication that his sole purpose for seeing her was to get her into the nearest bed. She chuckled wryly. Although if that had been his intent, they would have had a problem. They *did* have a problem. Where to go. Where to be alone. Her house, with her father present? His house, with his daughter present? Or a rendezvous at the hotel in Styx Switch that half the county would know about before they even completed their furtive coupling?

But if sex wasn't his main purpose for seeing her, what was? Phil was a busy man; the demands on his time were every bit as great as those on hers. Still, he made time to see her and made sure that he didn't interfere with her work.

Victoria knew they could talk together easily, but too often their conversations were limited to the nuts and bolts of cattle and careers. She knew she was not an unattractive woman but there had been little opportunity for her to truly look her best since the day of the party.

No, their times had been limited to quick cups of coffee after school at the Korner Kaff, which was all but deserted at that time of the day, or here at the ranch, with him accompanying her as she went about her chores. One day she had made a disparaging comment about how barn sour and out of shape their two horses were becoming, and Phil had suggested they ride the pastures, rather than driving the truck. As though aware of Zack's proprietorial concern for his horse, Phil hadn't even offered to ride him. Instead, he had begun trailering his own horse out to the ranch, giving Victoria the opportunity to rotate between exercising her mare and her father's gelding.

It wasn't enough for him. Victoria knew that. And no matter how much she enjoyed their times together, she wanted more, too.

A blue jay squawked a warning, a squirrel in one of the scattered oaks chattered angrily at a calf that had wandered under that tree, and Victoria brought herself back to the job at hand and studied the nearby herd. A couple of cows were close to their time, but none were in labor, and none showed signs of distress, although she made a mental note to keep an especially close watch on an eight-year-old Brahma cross.

The calves... In spite of the hope she still tried to hold on to, Pop was probably right about the bull. He usually was right, uncannily so, in matters of livestock. Too bad that sixth sense of his had been taking a nap when they'd plunked down money they couldn't afford to spend and jeopardized this year's crop.

Only one calf showed the size and weight for its age she expected to see: a white Limousin cross, standing beside the yellow replacement cow they had bought that fall. And that cow had been bred before they bought her. Bred. Dropped a fine calf. So she had obviously been sold because of her rotten disposition.

Victoria sighed and then smiled to herself in loving resignation. Pop didn't claim to be perfect, just right.

She looked at the sky again, noting the position of the sun, and giving herself a mental shake. She still had number three pasture to check, and Phil was picking her up tonight for a date. A real, Saturday night, dress up and go to town date.

She hurried back to the truck. What did he want from her? She still didn't know. She did know what she wanted from him, but that was an impossible dream. So for the time they had together, she'd give what she could, take what he offered, and tonight, maybe, she'd figure out what that was.

A WILCOX CAR waited when Victoria arrived back at the house, breathless, pressed for time, and wanting nothing more than a luxurious soak in a hot bath and a few minutes to adjust from the role of cowhand to that of dinner companion, before Phil came to pick her up. She patted the hood of Angela's car as she circled the front of it, knowing with a grim sense of foreboding that her plans had just been shot and wondering what had brought the girl out to the ranch. Except for a few times in the hall at school, she had not seen Angela since the night of her birthday party.

For a moment she hesitated, questioning whether the shocked expression she had seen on the girl's face that night and her impending date with Angela's father was what had finally brought her back to the ranch. *Go on in,* she urged herself. *You'll never find out, standing out here.*

Victoria let herself into the house through the kitchen, where she tugged off her boots and left them standing on a mat by the door. She heard voices from the living room and then laughter: Pop's, full-bodied, vibrant, as she hadn't heard it in ages, and Angela's, softer, conspiratorial and just as delighted.

Curious, she walked across the kitchen in her sock-clad feet and looked into the living room. They were seated on the couch: Pop, relaxed, but still exercising the old-fashioned formal manners he always extended to any female; Angela, cross-legged beside him.

For a moment Victoria stood silently, enjoying the sight of them oblivious to anyone or anything other than the pleasure they were so innocently sharing. Then she recognized the book Zack held open between them, a scrapbook Victoria's mother had lovingly compiled, and recognized the words her father spoke. He was telling tales.

Victoria leaned against the door, feeling a soft smile steal across her face as she listened to his words. His stories had delighted her as a child, had delighted anyone who came in contact with them. Stories of him as a young man in a wild country; stories of his father, his grandfather, cattlemen for generations—except for the few who were lawmen, or outlaws. She shook her head slowly, in love and reminiscence. And he was the last of them. A man born after his time. A man who should be as free and unfettered as the horses he had once tamed, as the land he had always loved. *Johnny Mack Brown, eat your heart out,* she thought. *Tex Ritter, here is the man you should have taken lessons from.*

Zack turned a page in the scrapbook. "This is me and my brother," he told Angela. "In front of some corrals we'd just built. And in the background, well, you can almost tell by looking how different things were there."

"But you loved it," Angela said softly.

"Yeah. Well, I guess I did. But, Lord, girl, that picture's got to be close to fifty years old. Victoria's mama, she was a Southern girl. She got to missing trees and hills. I couldn't see myself as a Southerner, but this place was close enough for her. She loved it here, like Vickie does." He reached out and touched the photograph. "But there... there a man could see forever."

Victoria heard the pain in his voice when he talked about her mother, when he talked about the days before his stroke. *No stress,* the doctors had said. And what constituted stress, she wondered. Physical pain, or emotional? She straightened to her full five feet five inches and fixed a smile on her face. "Hi there."

Angela looked up, startled, and a flush worked its way over her face. "Oh. Hi."

For the first time Victoria noticed the unfamiliar garment bag draped over the back of the couch. She cast a questioning glance at it, then back at Angela. "Run away from home?"

Angela's flush deepened. In a flurry of activity, she untangled her too-long legs, rose from the couch and tugged at the hem of her bright purple sweatshirt. "No. That is—" Her mouth twisted uncertainly. "Could we talk? Just the two of us?"

"Of course." Victoria hoped her confusion wasn't as obvious as the girl's. "My room?"

Angela nodded. She looked down at Zack still seated on the couch. "Thanks, Mr. Tankersley. I really enjoyed this afternoon. Maybe we could... Maybe we could do it again sometime?"

Zack looked up at her, surprise and pleasure evident on his face. "Maybe. If you're sure you're not just humoring an old man."

"No," Angela told him. "I'm—" She glanced at Victoria and snatched up the garment bag. "Thanks again," she said before hurrying from the room.

Victoria walked to her father's side and dropped a hand onto his shoulder. The scrapbook lay opened to a picture of a much younger Zack, a still younger Ted, and a vast expanse of range land. *A land where you can see forever.* She had seen forever that afternoon, and she hadn't particularly liked what she saw, but she couldn't tell her father that. Gently she closed the album. "Flatlander," she said, grinning cheekily at him, seeking and receiving an answering grin to a long-standing debate. "What good does it do to see forever, if there's nothing to look at?"

WHEN VICTORIA ENTERED her bedroom and closed the door behind her, Angela stopped her restless pacing and stood hesitantly near the foot of the bed where she had draped the garment bag.

Victoria resisted the urge to look at the bedside clock. She leaned against the door and waited for Angela to speak. When it became obvious that Angela wouldn't, or couldn't broach the subject, she stifled a sigh. "What did you want to talk about?" she prompted softly.

"Ah . . ." Angela lifted her face toward the ceiling. "You're—you're going out with Dad tonight."

Victoria felt her muscles tighten and the first surge of adrenaline as her body prepared itself for confrontation. She willed herself to relax. A woman, even one as young as Angela, didn't carry a garment bag with her to warn another woman off. "Yes," Victoria said softly, then voiced the question that hung between them. "Do you have a problem with that?"

"No!" Angela answered too quickly. She sighed. "I did have. Until Dad set me straight." She smiled wryly. "Chewed me out, is what he did."

"Angela, I certainly never meant to come between—"

"You didn't." She hung her head. "I did. And everything's fine between us now, honest it is. And I've apologized to him for barging in on you two that night. I thought it would be enough, but it wasn't, not for me. I know how embarrassed you were, but I didn't know how to say anything to you before now. Still don't."

She turned to the garment bag and began unzipping it. "I sew. I guess you knew that from what Miss Bailey said about costumes. I'm good at it. I thought maybe if I couldn't convince you by telling you how sorry I was for that night, and how I really don't have a problem with your being Dad's friend, too, I could *show* you, by designing something just for you."

Angela stopped her fumbling with the zipper and sank onto the bed, hanging her head. "This was so much easier when I was planning it," she admitted. "I mean, the design just came to me, and I knew it was you. I didn't think about how hard *explaining* all this was going to be."

Victoria left her protected place at the door and walked across the room to the young woman. "And I haven't given you much help, have I?"

Angela shook her head. "Are you still mad at me?"

"Oh, Angela, I never was mad at you. At myself, maybe. But not at you." Victoria raised hesitant fingers toward the zipper of the bag. "No one ever designed a dress for me before." Whatever was inside the bag—and with Angela's penchant for far-out style and outlandish colors, it could be anything—Victoria knew she would treasure it because of the way it came to be. She raised the zipper and stood staring at the dress. "Oh, Angela."

"You don't like it?"

Victoria closed her eyes and sighed before reaching to caress the dress. The color of old lace, it had a dozen tiny covered buttons running up the fitted bodice to a high collar, and lined insets of the same old lace it resembled. "It's beautiful." She lifted it from the bag and held it against herself. "But you don't really see me this way, do you?" she asked, because although the dress was almost starkly simple in design, without a frill, flounce, or ruffle, it was the most feminine garment she had ever seen.

Angela appeared not to have heard her question. "I've got a good eye for size," she said, "but I brought needle and thread in case we have to make a few alterations. I didn't think about underwear and shoes...."

Victoria smiled, still caressing the dress, and remembered her little-used wardrobe. "I can manage."

"Good." Angela's confidence seemed to have returned. "If you'd try it on, I could make any changes while you bathe. I know you're jammed for time, and I want to get out of here before Dad shows up."

"Tonight? You want me to wear this tonight?"

"You *don't* like it," Angela said, reaching for the dress. "Okay, so it was a dumb idea."

"No." Victoria hugged the dress to her and took a cautious step forward. "It was a wonderful idea. And I'd be crazy not to like this dress." Crazy to like it, too, because if she'd felt like a fraud in the blue silk dress the night of Angela's birthday, how would she feel in this ivory and lace creation?

WHEN VICTORIA EMERGED from the bathroom quite a while later, clad in a comfortable blue terry-cloth robe, her freshly shampooed hair dried and hanging in loose waves almost to her waist, she heard the muffled sounds of laughter coming from the kitchen.

She made her way quietly through the small house and stood in the kitchen doorway. The remains of her father's meal had been pushed to one side of the table in front of him. Angela sat in Victoria's chair, elbows propped on the table as she listened with rapt attention to what he was saying. She made a quiet comment, too soft for Victoria to hear, and the two of them burst into conspiratorial laughter.

Victoria felt a quick stab of— Surely not jealousy, she told herself, fighting back a suspicious lump in her throat. She knew her father loved her, knew that the two of them shared a closeness that had been made even more intense by their working together, knew that they each held a special place in the other's heart. But how long had it been since he had looked at *her* with the gentle affection he now showed Angela? And how long had it been, that afternoon's coerced grin notwithstanding, since she had brought a smile to his face, let alone coaxed him into laughter?

She felt her shoulders slumping, dragging her posture down to the same dejected level as her thoughts. Wallowing, her mother would have called it. It was something she still didn't have time for, and something she found herself doing too much of lately. She forced herself to stand erect, forced her wayward thoughts from the path they seemed bent on taking.

Angela was being kind to them. Victoria recognized that and appreciated it.

Another adolescent girl might have been much more protective of her father and less understanding of his dating a woman so different from what she thought he needed; Angela had all but given her blessing. And Victoria was jealous of the few minutes of pleasure the girl gave *her* father? Besides, she told herself, shaking her head defiantly, although they had not had much laughter the past few years, they had at least had the years. And they would have more. Many more. She would see to that.

She stepped into the kitchen, smiling, and reached to take the dishes from the table. "Thanks, Angela," she said, recognizing from the food that it was something beyond her father's camp fire cooking skills. "You didn't have to do that."

"Oh, I didn't mind." Angela scrambled up from the chair and intercepted Victoria's reach for the dishes. "You go on and get dressed. And I'll scoot out of here just as soon as I take care of this little dab of dishes. Honest," she said when Victoria hesitated, "and you're almost out of time."

"You're as bad as your mama sometimes, Vickie," Zack said gruffly, pushing out of his chair. "You'd think nobody knew how to do anything but you. I'll do the dishes."

She bit back a quick denial, because dancing in his eyes was the look she had just been complaining about missing. And she restrained an equally quick laugh. *As bad as her mother?* She might argue about having inherited that trait—she wasn't sure she had—but if she had, the genes that carried it hadn't come from her mother. Chuckling softly, she admitted defeat and

with a few quick words of thanks left her father and
Angela to sort out the dishes.

THE APPRECIATIVE LOOK in Phil's eyes when he
picked her up that evening erased the doubts that had
first plagued Victoria when she put on the dress, arranged her hair in a loose Gibson Girl style and
stepped into the new bone-colored pumps she had
bought that spring. And she knew that her look as she
quietly studied him had to be just as approving.
Wearing a dark blue suit with a dress shirt of lighter
blue, which complemented the richness of his red hair
and beard and darkened his eyes, he seemed larger,
more imposing, more out of reach than ever.

With only a few polite words to Zack, Phil hurried
Victoria out of the kitchen and into his car. At the base
of their hill, he stopped the car and turned to her,
lightly tracing her cheek with his fingertips and giving
her a gentle kiss. He sighed and sank back into his
seat. "Just checking to see if you're real," he said, "or
a vision conjured up by my overactive imagination."

Victoria swallowed back a suspicious lump in her
throat. "Well," she asked lightly, "which am I?"

He put the car in gear and pulled out onto the road
before covering her hand with his. "Oh, you're real,
lady. Too real." He squeezed her hand. "Although
tonight, I may have to keep checking."

Their destination that night was Fort Smith, Ar-
kansas, a little over an hour's drive away, and the
Lighthouse Restaurant, on the bank of the Arkansas
River, where they hopefully wouldn't run into more
than a half dozen or so persons from Hillsboro or Styx
Switch.

They were early for their reservation and rather than risk spoiling the mood that had surrounded their drive by waiting in the adjoining lounge, Victoria opted for a quiet walk on the wooden deck that fronted the river side of the restaurant. The air was chilly, but pleasantly so, carrying the promise of spring. She walked to the edge of the deck, bracing her hands on the rail, and looked out over the river.

Phil stood behind her, his arms on either side of her sheltering her from the breeze and enveloping her with his warmth. "Lean back," he urged. "It has to be too cool for you."

Victoria shook her head. "Besides," she said, remembering the walls of glass behind them, "we're in full view of all the people in the dining room."

"And they aren't paying any more attention to us than we are to them."

Phil stepped closer, and, with a sigh, Victoria leaned back against his chest, feeling the steady rhythm of his heartbeat and breathing as he enveloped her with his strength. Across the wide expanse of the river, she could see the lights of Van Buren, once the starting place for thousands of immigrants on their westward journey, now a quiet small city undergoing renovation. In the river channel a coal-laden barge accompanied by tugboats made its way south toward the Mississippi. A gaily pennanted houseboat was tied up below them at the restaurant's dock.

"I'm glad they reopened the waterway," she said.

Phil's hand had left its place on the railing, found her arm, and was now making its way up and down, gently caressing, sending spirals of warmth through her and lighting delicious little tingles along its path. "Locks and dams and tugboats included?"

"Mmm." She turned her cheek against his chest. "But I wish there were the paddleboats, too. The steamers that used to travel this river."

"You're a romantic, Victoria Tankersley," he chided gently.

"No. I *was*." The denial came too easily, and Victoria wondered briefly how many times she had convinced herself of it to have sounded so matter-of-fact. "But not anymore." Except tonight, she thought. Tonight, she felt like a romantic. Tonight there were no pressures, except those of two people who were drawn to each other.

A brightly lighted pleasure boat passed them, and laughter drifted over the water. "But sometimes," she admitted, sighing, "sometimes I wonder what it would be like to get on one of those boats, to go south, to the Mississippi, to New Orleans, to the Gulf. To just keep on going."

"You'd come back," he told her.

For the first time Victoria let herself wonder what would have happened if all her dreams of so long ago had come true. Would she have been happy? She'd been sure then that she would be. But now—now she'd never know. And she'd never really know how she would have responded to Phil's statement had her life not taken such a dramatic turn. The only thing she could be sure of was how she felt at this moment.

"Yes." She dropped her head, then raised it and turned to look at him. "Yes, I would. This is home." The lush green hills and the valley where she had grown up, the ranch that was so much a part of her, and this man, although she knew she couldn't tell him, this man who had barged into her life and refused to leave her alone, all of these things were home to her.

DINNER WAS SERVED at an intimate table for two, arranged to give the impression of a private dining room. It consisted of the fresh lobster and crab legs Phil had promised her, accompanied by candlelight, wine and a pleasurable tension-filled sense of expectancy.

Afterward they walked arm in arm across the parking lot, lost in the isolation of the location in spite of the cars that surrounded them and enjoying the night breeze that carried the faint scent of fresh, moving water. Phil opened the car door for her and then leaned down after she had scooted into the seat. "I don't want to take you home yet."

She looked up at him. His face was highlighted by moonlight, and the uncertainty she saw caught her breath in her throat. "No," she whispered. "Not yet."

Phil turned off the highway at a newly built hotel. He guided her through the lobby with a firm hand on her back to the hotel lounge, a small, uncrowded room. They ordered drinks, sipped from them, made attempts at small talk, and the expectancy grew.

Phil reached for her hand and clasped it. "Dance with me."

On the tiny dance floor, Victoria went into his arms easily, amazed at how well their bodies fit together despite the difference in height. The music was soft and dreamy, the steps nothing that would ever win a dance contest, but Victoria was lost in the magic of it all, and in the spell of the man who held her with such gentle possessiveness.

The music stopped, began again, and again, and still they danced. The muted noises from the bar, the occasional soft laugh or murmur of conversation from the room around them, all of these things faded. There was only the brush of thigh against thigh, breast against chest, the kiss of Phil's breath across her cheek, and their softly whispered words, until Phil came to a stop in a dark corner of the dance floor and stood holding her in his arms.

She felt the tension in him and the arousal he had not spoken of, for some reason would not speak of. What did he want from her? She still did not know. But right now, at this moment, he wanted her as much as she wanted him.

She looked up at him, tracing her fingers across his beard until she found the softness of his lips. And there was something else she knew. The moment had come. Whether Phil spoke the words, or she, they had to be said. "Don't you think—don't you think it's time for you to see about getting us a room?"

She heard his ragged intake of breath before he pulled her closer. "Are you sure?"

She nodded her head against his chest, feeling the heavy beat of his heart. "I'm sure."

His answer was to squeeze her tightly, then release her and lead her back to their table. He met her eyes when he seated her, and in his she read yearning and a desire so intense it would have frightened her had he been anyone other than Phil. "Wait here," he said hoarsely. "I won't be gone long."

THE ROOM was pseudo-French Provincial, bathed in the soft light of the lamp that glowed to life when Phil flipped the switch by the door before turning to twist the night lock into place. Victoria stood just inside the door, looking at the two cabriole-legged chairs flanking a small table, at the television bolted to a brace halfway up the wall, at the king-sized bed that dominated the room.

She felt Phil's hands drop onto her shoulders and twisted her head to look up at him.

"It's almost clinically impersonal, isn't it?" he asked bleakly.

"It's clean," she told him, turning to face him. "It's new. And it's *private*."

He chuckled at the emphasis she put on private, but almost immediately his eyes darkened. He lifted his hands to cradle her face. "Victoria, I've wanted you for so long, but I wanted our first time to be special for you. More special than an hour stolen from something else you should have been doing. More special than the anonymity of a rented room."

"Phil..." She rested her cheek against the comfort of his palm. She loved this man. She couldn't deny it to herself any longer. But, God, the timing was wrong, all wrong. There wasn't enough of her to share with anything, with anyone else. Not yet. Maybe not for years. She looked into his eyes, willing him to understand. *Please don't ask me for any more than this,* she pleaded silently. *I haven't any more to give. Please don't want any more.*

She lifted her fingers to his beard, smiling hesitantly. "I wondered about your beard," she said softly. "The first night we went to dinner. I wondered how it would feel to touch it, to have it touching me."

Groaning, he lifted her to him, covering her mouth with his and showing her the hunger she had seen in his eyes. Victoria's hands went around his neck, one to the back of his head where her fingers found the silky softness of his hair, the other to his shoulder where she found the strength of muscle hidden by his tailored suit, and she answered Phil's hunger with her own, too long denied.

He pulled away from her, breathing raggedly, released his grip on her, and rested his hand on her ribs, just below her breast. "I'll hurt you."

Victoria looked up at him, dazed and confused.

"If I'm not careful, I'll hurt you," he repeated. He lifted his other hand to her throat. "I'm not supposed to admit it, I know. But I've never felt so clumsy, so awkward in my life."

And I've never felt so fragile, so cherished. Thank you, she thought. *Thank you for this.*

She covered his hand on her throat with one of her own. "You could never be clumsy or awkward," she told him, "and you would never hurt me."

She guided his hand to the row of buttons that began at her throat and lifted her hands to the knot of his tie. "Don't you think it's time?"

"God, yes. I've wanted to do this all night."

She looked down to where his strong hand now rested, over her heart, at his long fingers fumbling with the tiny buttons. As she watched, she saw his hand tremble.

"What devious mind thought up this way to tempt and torture a man?"

Victoria laughed softly. Later she would tell him, but not now. Now there was no room in their private world for his daughter, for her father, for clients, cattle, debts or students. Now there was room only for the two of them, Phil and Victoria, exploring and discovering each other's bodies as she had already explored his mind and heart.

She tugged his tie loose from its knot and with her own shaking fingers began the tantalizing process of separating the buttons on his shirt. She spread the shirt open. The same luxurious hair that covered his head, his face, that peeked from the collar of his shirt, covered his chest in a tight, curly mat. She slid her fingers across the expanse of his chest, closing her eyes, not looking at him again until she felt him part her dress.

He drew a finger across her breast, tracing the edge of her lace camisole, once again trembling. "Lord," he whispered, "I'm glad I didn't know until now that *this* was what you were wearing underneath all those buttons."

She dropped her arms to her sides, letting him push the dress off her shoulders and past her hips. He bent to her, tracing the line of lace across her breast with his lips. Victoria felt the soft brush of his mustache against her skin, the moist warmth of his breath and his mouth inflaming the need that had been building within her for weeks, felt a moan break free, wordlessly voicing that need. She lifted her hands to his neck, leaning against him, holding him to her.

"It's time," he whispered hoarsely against her throat. "Oh, yes, Victoria," he said, picking her up and carrying her to the bed. "It definitely is time."

VICTORIA AWOKE from a sleep of sated exhaustion to find herself pressed chest to thigh against Phil. She stretched lightly and contentedly, feeling the play of different textures of flesh, muscle and hair against one another. She felt a flush stealing over her as she remembered how that flesh and muscle had moved earlier, how uninhibitedly she had taken everything he had so graciously and gracefully given, but even the memory of her actions, her hunger, her greed couldn't destroy the euphoria she still felt.

In sleep they had continued to cling to each other. Now her hand rested lightly on his chest, her fingers twined in the rough mat of curls that covered it. She had never thought much about hairy-chested men before, never bought in to the macho theory that chest hair denoted masculinity. With Phil, though, she might have to reconsider. Of course, it was just a part of him, like the warmth his body exuded even at rest, his strength, his always surprising gentleness. But she had to admit there was something erotic about the feel of that mat of hair against her, or beneath her cheek. She let her fingers drift upward to his jaw. And there was something definitely erotic about his beard. She felt herself warming at the memories flooding through her. More erotic than she had ever imagined.

She twisted her head slightly, looking up. Phil was awake, watching her. As her eyes met his, his expression lightened. "If we don't leave soon," he said, beginning a delicate tracing of his own over her hip and thigh, "it will be dawn before I get you home."

Victoria felt a stab of unwarranted despair at leaving him. He had given her more than she had dreamed of, and not just physically, although she knew that was all they could have. But she didn't want it to end, not yet. She didn't want to leave this room, impersonal though it was, because here at least she could maintain the illusion that she was free to love, free to accept what her heart, for this moment, wanted to think Phil offered. What they had shared tonight was wonderful, but not enough. Would it ever be enough? "Now?" she asked.

"No." Phil smoothed his hand up her side to cup her breast before gathering her closer to his warmth. "Not yet. It's still tonight." He turned, bending over her, holding her tightly against him. "And tonight, all of it, is ours."

Chapter Eight

Except for the small fluorescent light they always left on over the kitchen sink, Phil's house was dark as he turned into his driveway in the predawn grayness. Victoria's house had been even darker.

She had laughed softly at his suggestion that he stick around, or come back in a half hour or so to help feed the cattle. "My father's not going to take a horse-whip to me, or a shotgun to you," she teased gently in the low tones the darkness seemed to demand, "but don't you think we'd defeat the purpose of all this stealth if you show up to feed the livestock in a suit and dress shoes?"

She was right. Of course she was right. He knew that. But he hadn't wanted to leave her. He hadn't wanted to take her home at all.

Phil parked in front of the garage and sat looking at his dark house. Dark and lonely. He sighed and slumped back in the car seat. Could he honestly call his house lonely with Angela filling it with her adolescent antics and friends, with family constantly dropping by, with clients tying up the telephone lines? Yes, he could, he admitted. Now. Now that he knew what was missing.

For a while tonight that hotel room, as impersonal as it was, had been more home than the house he had lived in for the past fifteen years. He closed his eyes. It hadn't been the room; it had been the woman. For a while tonight, she had shed her armor and had let herself be the woman he had only glimpsed before: soft, vulnerable, giving. God, so giving.

He hadn't wanted to take her home. He still didn't. Right now, he wanted to be back in that room, held by her with silken and velvet ties he doubted she believed existed. He wanted to be joined with her, to lie with her in the aftermath of loving.

He hadn't been as gentle with her the first time as he had meant to be. With her responses, control had fled. Afterward he had lain holding her, stunned by the intensity of what they had shared. The emotions of protectiveness and possessiveness, as much as his depleted physical state, had kept him still. He'd lifted his hand to her cheek and found her silent tears. "I did hurt you," he began. "I—"

"No." Her soft, husky denial interrupted him. "No." She wiped at her tears and then as though realizing how ineffectual that was, burrowed closer to him, holding him.

Phil opened his eyes and looked at his dark house, distinct now against the light gray of the sky. Impossibly he felt again the ache of wanting her. He stepped from his car and eased the door closed, chuckling at his actions in spite of himself. He wasn't a teenager, sneaking into his house after staying out way past curfew, but there was no sense in making more noise than absolutely necessary. And while Victoria had seemed certain that Zack wouldn't greet them with a horsewhip and shotgun, Phil wasn't at all sure what Angela's reaction would be.

He let himself into the dark house equally quietly. He and Victoria had not mentioned love, or commitment, or the future. He would have, if she had given him any indication she was ready to hear what he had to say. Instead she had seemed almost desperate to keep what they had shared on a physical level. That wasn't going to be possible. Phil knew that, with a certainty he hadn't felt in years. He'd find a way to help her out of this mess she was in. He'd find a way to convince her that where she really belonged was at his side. And then there would be no need for stealth, his or hers.

Grinning confidently, he headed for the kitchen. There was no sense in going to bed at this hour. After a couple of cups of coffee, he'd be able to take care of some necessary work and then get down to the business of resolving his future.

Still grinning, he pushed open the kitchen door. The red light on the coffee maker grinned back at him from across the room. He stopped in midstride. His daughter sat at the kitchen table, wrapped in one of his old bathrobes, holding a cup of coffee. A notebook and pencil rested by her elbow. Angela looked up at him, not smiling. "You always told me to call if I was going to be late."

BY TEN O'CLOCK, Victoria was regretting her lack of sleep, but not enough to have foregone the night before. She caught Zack looking at her strangely a couple of times during the morning and suspected that he knew to the minute what time she had come in and had a pretty good idea of what she had been doing. But he didn't say anything. For that she was grateful. She didn't want to have to defend her actions; she wasn't too sure they were defendable.

And she didn't want to examine them. Not yet. But as the morning wore on and she went about her chores, as little-used muscles protested, as lack of sleep grained her eyes, she found herself remembering them. In fragments. Maybe she should be ashamed of her wantonness of the night before. She didn't think so; it had felt too right at the time. But she didn't know. She hadn't had a close woman friend to share things with in ten years, not since Leah at college, and then Victoria had been reluctant to discuss Brad with her. One didn't talk about one's lover to his sister. One didn't talk about one's lover at all, according to Victoria's mother. What happens between a man and a woman is special to them, her mother had told her long ago. It's not something to be picked apart, gossiped over, or bragged about. Not if you care for each other. And if you don't care enough to keep the relationship sacred to the two of you, you don't care enough to be intimate.

The yellow cow lowered her head and glared at Victoria as she stepped down from the truck in number two pasture, and Victoria glared back. She wasn't foolish enough to try to make pets out of her cattle, she'd known better than that almost as long as she'd known how to walk, but most of them identified her as a source of food and at least tolerated her presence. Not that one. That one, idiotic as it might seem to anyone else, seemed locked in a constant battle of wills with Victoria, determined that she would be in control. Victoria didn't need that. Too much in her life was spinning out of control. Pop, constantly trying to assume too much responsibility in spite of his health, getting more lost in the memories of his youth. Her emotions, seesawing up and down when she thought about Phil Wilcox. Even the weather. She glanced up at the low clouds scudding across the gray morning sky and shivered in her light jacket as she realized how much the temperature had dropped.

What did Phil want from her, she asked herself again as she turned away from the yellow cow and began scanning the herd. She'd asked that question standing in this same place the day before and thought that by now she'd know the answer. Maybe she did. She hoped she did. She hugged herself against the chill and against the memories of the night before. He knew she wasn't able to make any long-term commitment. As busy as he was, as tied up with family and his clients, maybe he wasn't able to do that, either. They were good together; that was undeniable. Maybe, like her, he needed someone to help him through days and nights that were too full of work, too empty of caring. Maybe he just needed someone to help him fend off Angela's matchmaking.

Who was she kidding? Not herself. She needed so much more from Phil than an interlude. But she couldn't give him any more than that. She felt tears on her cheeks and swiped at them angrily. She never cried. Never. Crying was a sign of weakness, and she couldn't afford to be weak.

She took a deep breath, blinking back her tears, willing them to stop, and renewed her search.

She found the red Brahma-cross cow away from the herd, in a small grove of trees. To refer to her as an eight-year-old was a kindness to the animal. Cattle were aged by their teeth. After eight years, correctly aging one was a matter of guesswork, or careful record keeping. Five years earlier this cow had been recorded as an eight-year-old. She should probably have been sold long before, but she was a dependable breeder, dropped and weaned a good calf every year, with no problems. Victoria walked toward the cow, who looked at her and sidled farther into the trees. Victoria stopped and spoke softly. "It's okay, lady. I'm not going to bother you."

She glanced again at the sky. The clouds were thicker now, the sky a pale gray. Snow. The March snow that always seemed to surprise the townspeople never surprised the ranchers. The rancher's question was never, "Will it snow?" but "How much?" How much today, Victoria didn't know. Her first impulse, given the sky and the old cow in labor, was to hurry back to the house for her horse and dogs and move the animal to shelter. How Pop would hoot at that. And rationally she knew he was right. This cow would probably calve before Victoria could get her to the barn.

And he would hoot at what she planned to do instead. Wait. Wait for a cow that had successfully delivered at least ten calves to give birth to another one. Wait and hope that the cow had this one delivered, licked dry and nursing before the first snowflake fell. An hour? Probably no longer than that. She tried to tell herself it was an hour she didn't have to waste; her accounts were waiting for her and the classroom assignments she still had to grade and her own school work.

She walked closer, crooning softly, snatched up a blade of tall winter grass near the base of an oak and leaned against the tree, idly shredding the grass as she silently watched and encouraged the cow. Birthing was not an uncommon experience to her. Cows, horses, dogs, cats, all multiplied on a ranch, and none of the process had ever been kept secret from her. And she had never become inured to it. The miracle of birth fascinated her, the miracle of giving life and nurturing it.

Victoria felt an emptiness within her, an ache of longing so intense it shook her. Would she ever know this miracle? She was nearing thirty now, and while thirty wasn't ancient, how old would she be when she could finally think of marrying, think of starting a family? Would she ever hold a baby of her own? If she did—Victoria closed her eyes and dropped the blade of grass—if she did, the baby wouldn't have red hair and gray eyes. And if she didn't—

"Damn!" she said softly, feeling tears on her cheeks again. She wouldn't cry. She *wouldn't*. She'd made her choices long ago, and she had her reward. Pop. Alive. Proud again. And as healthy as could be expected. And it was worth it. Sighing, she stooped to pick another blade of grass and seated herself at the base of the tree, remembering how he had been only a few short years before. Oh, yes. It was worth it.

PHIL STARTED THE MORNING at the sheriff's office, spent several uncomfortable minutes with Sam Hastings, and then went to the hospital where things didn't get better. Sam's telephone call at three o'clock in the morning was what had awakened Angela. Will had run out of the house in the middle of an argument with his father, taken the truck without permission, attempted to outrace a deputy sheriff who tried to stop him for speeding and had wrecked the truck. Now Will was in the hospital with a half dozen charges hanging over him, and Sam was the picture of a confused and troubled father. But Phil wished he had seen Will before he talked to Sam.

Will was seventeen years old, almost an adult in the eyes of the law. He was also almost six feet tall, darkly handsome in a way that appealed to more girls at the local high school than Phil liked to think about, and looked older than his years. He was belligerent, antagonistic and obnoxious most of the time. Hardly the stereotype of the vulnerable, battered child.

Except today. He was asleep when Phil entered the room, all pale bandages and pallid skin against the sterile white sheets. He had a broken arm, two broken ribs, a cut over his left eye, a split lip, and more bruises than Phil thought it possible for that rattletrap of a truck to give him.

Will opened his unswollen eye and looked at Phil, and in that brief glance Phil felt himself being examined and weighed as he knew all adults were in Will's eyes. "Sam send you to bail his boy out again?" Will asked.

"Something like that." Phil pulled the room's one chair close to the bed and sat down, placing himself at eye level with the boy. "You want to tell me your version of what happened?"

"Why should I?" Will asked emotionlessly. "You've already read the police reports and talked to my dad."

"And looked at your truck," Phil told him. "As bad as it is, it's hard to see how it did all that damage to you."

Will closed his eye and turned his head on the pillow so that he faced the ceiling. "What do you want me to say? Admit that I was in a fight last night? That'll sound real good when we go to court, won't it?"

"It might help explain why you did what you did. You're still a juvenile, Will. Lots of factors will be considered when we go in for your hearing. And there's not much chance that we're going to get out of having one now. Did you have a fight last night?" And who with? Phil wanted to ask. In spite of Sam's apparent concern, that question still bothered Phil, as did the "resisting arrest" charge lodged by Will's uncle. The condition Will was in indicated that he wouldn't have been able to attempt to resist anything after the wreck, but he could sense Will's defense mechanisms working and didn't want to plant any escape route in the boy's mind. "Where did you get all those bruises, Will?" he asked instead. "And where did you get the beer?"

"I wasn't drunk," Will said steadily, without looking at him.

"I know. The hospital had to take a blood sample before they could give you any medication. But you had been drinking."

"So," Will said companionably, "I rat on a friend and maybe I save myself some grief?"

"No." Was there any way to reach him? Phil didn't know. At that moment, he wasn't even sure why he was trying, other than a nagging suspicion that all was not what it seemed. "No. But maybe, if I knew all the circumstances, I could figure out the best course of action to take for you."

Will twisted on the pillow, grimacing against the pain of sudden movement. "Best for me? Seems like I've heard that before." His lips pulled back in a snarl.

"You do that, Wilcox. You do that. Just as soon as you figure out what that is."

"BEST FOR HIM." Phil's mind played with the subtle twist of meaning Will had given his words as he drove his pickup south. The problem was, he didn't know what was best for anyone: best for Will, best for Sam, best for Victoria, best for himself. He shook his head. Must be the lack of sleep, he thought, fogging up his brain, but he knew better. He wasn't old enough, yet, for one sleepless night to destroy his thinking processes. He knew what was best for him, and although only a few hours had passed since he left her on her porch, he knew he had to see her again.

The first snowflake hit his windshield as he turned into the Tankersley drive. By the time he reached the top of the hill, the flakes were falling steadily, big, wet snowflakes that hit the windshield in globs and melted as soon as they touched the warm glass.

He didn't see the Tankersley truck at the house, and for the first time, he wondered if he should have called. Zack could be the one who was gone, out making his regular rounds, but that thought was dispelled when Victoria's father stepped out of the nearest barn, carrying a bridle and accompanied by the two dogs. Phil got out of his truck and walked to meet the old man.

"Guess you're here to see Vickie," Zack said, looking at him in the disconcerting way he had. Almost, Phil thought, as though he were boring into his mind, examining the thoughts he found there, and then backing out, never giving any indication if what he found pleased or displeased him.

"Yes." Phil did see something in the man's eyes. Angela wasn't the only one who knew what time they'd gotten home that morning. And Zack probably knew about something that Angela didn't. That last kiss, on the porch, the one that neither one of them had wanted to end. He waited for the inevitable question.

Zack glanced down at the bridle in his hand, then back at Phil. "She's up in number two pasture. Should have been back by now. I don't suppose you'd mind driving up there and seeing if she needs a hand with something, would you?"

Phil didn't delude himself that Zack was giving any sort of blessing to his pursuit of Victoria. No, it was more like the jury was still out in the man's mind, and until he was more sure of his own thoughts, he wouldn't voice any of them. But that was enough for Phil, for now. "No. I wouldn't mind at all."

He found Victoria's truck with no trouble, and when he parked beside it, looking over the pasture, he saw her, standing near a small clump of oak trees that were just beginning to bud into leaf. She waved at him, motioning him to silence as he stepped from his truck, so he eased the door closed rather than slamming it, before walking to her side.

Instead of melting, the snow was beginning to stick to the ground now in little patches between the upthrust of dried grass and new green. Some of it had filtered through the still-bare branches of the tree to dust her dark hair and the shoulders of her jacket. God, she was beautiful, he thought.

As naturally as breathing, he reached for her. She stepped away, as though unaware of his intent, or unwilling for him to embrace her, and with a tightening in his throat he recognized the proud set of her shoulders, her erect posture. Her armor was back. "Problems?" he asked.

"No." She nodded toward her left, ignoring his real question, and he followed the direction she indicated. They stood a respectful distance from a cow busily cleaning a newborn calf. "For a while I was afraid there might be," she went on in a carefully neutral voice. "It took her longer than I thought it should. Fortunately the calf was small. They all are this year. Pop's planning on replacing the bull—"

"Victoria." He put his hand on her shoulder, silencing her. She'd been standing out in the snow, anticipating a difficult calving, by herself. She needed help. He could help her. For a second, only a second, he thought about Will. Will knew enough to be a good cowhand, once his injuries healed, and with Phil paying his wages, he could bet on it. He could talk Victoria and Zack into it—he knew that—into bringing the boy here to live, getting him away from Sam and any possible threat until the truth of that situation could be learned, but would that really help her, or only make things worse? And right now, Will Hastings wasn't his major concern. Victoria was. He was losing her. He felt it, felt her slipping farther away from him as she withdrew into herself, and he didn't understand why.

He lifted his other hand to her cheek and tilted her face up, looking into her dark, troubled eyes. "I missed you," he said softly.

He felt her soft exhalation of breath as the tension left her, saw her eyes clear and her lips part in a welcoming smile. "And I missed you."

Yes, she definitely was what was best for him he thought as he bent to gather her to him, to cover that wonderful, loving mouth of hers with his own. Now all he had to do was convince her that he was what was best for her.

Chapter Nine

Victoria smiled and sank back in her chair as her after-hours tutoring pair left the classroom. If she had done nothing else worthy of note that semester, she had reached at least two of her students. Jimmie Foresman, Abigail's profanity-prone grandson, had actually asked for her help, and not just out of unrequited love for Lydia Benton. And Lydia, self-appointed critic of the freshman class, had unbent enough to share some of her knowledge as one of the tutor assistants in the program Victoria had tentatively proposed at the beginning of the semester. Not Jimmie's assistant. Victoria grinned. Although Jimmie would have loved that arrangement.

She rose, crossed to the windows and began closing them, shutting out the warm April air. The air carried more than the promise of spring; it carried spring itself into the high-ceilinged old classroom. No wonder the students had been restless that day; she had been restless herself.

Would Phil be there today? The day before, he had been kept late by a court case; the day before that, by an emergency with a client. Victoria closed the last window and leaned her head against the warm glass.

From the beginning they had been living on her time schedule; it was unconscionable for her, now, to resent the intrusion of his responsibilities. She wouldn't resent them. And she wouldn't feel guilty; guilty that he seemed to spend more time working with her on her place than he spent working on his own; guilty about the time that she stole from her work to be with him; guilty about their infrequent and furtive trips to Fort Smith; guilty that she was getting much more from their involvement than she was capable of giving.

She had to see him. It was as simple and as complex as that. Like breathing. Like her heartbeat. Like any other life-sustaining function. For as long as he wanted to be with her, she had to be with him, which wouldn't be long enough. Not if the restlessness she sensed in him and the dissatisfaction she occasionally glimpsed in the depths of his eyes were the indicators she feared they were. Neither one of them was the type for a secret affair. She should have known better a month ago when she deluded herself into believing that they were, or that what they had could be anything but just an affair. She didn't have the time or the energy for the open courtship that would be acceptable to his concerned family or to the openly curious interests of the townspeople, and she wasn't free to make the kind of commitment such a courtship implied.

Get ready to lose him, Victoria, she told herself. You always knew it was only a matter of time. But not yet, she pleaded silently. Not when they still had moments like they had shared the past weekend. It was well past time for her to be off horseback and onto the tractor, pulling the six-foot brush hog across the pastures, destroying the weeds and young saplings that always tried to encroach. Only a downed gap-gate and two missing cows had kept her from that bone-rattling chore.

Phil had gone with her, helped her find the cows and their calves high on the brush-covered hillside, had helped her drive them back to the herd, had helped her with makeshift repairs to the gate. Then, Phil had turned to her with a disquieting, hesitant smile. "Humor me," he said, heading his horse up the hill. He seldom asked her for anything, never asked, she realized in stunned silence. She had followed him, instead of returning to the house and to Pop as she knew she should, letting her mare pick its way up the narrow trail behind him, until he stopped at the bank of a small stream they had passed earlier. She knew that in a few weeks all that would remain of the stream would be a dusty, rock-walled gully, but now water bubbled over the pebbles in the creek bed, and wild flowers and grasses grew in colorful profusion.

Phil dismounted, but when Victoria started to do the same, he shook his head. "Wait. Please."

Puzzled, she twisted on the saddle, watching him as he tied his reins to an overhanging branch, took her reins from her and did the same with them. He lifted her foot from the stirrup and tugged her boot off.

"Phil?" she asked with a hesitant, shaky laugh as she felt the now familiar warmth of desire curling to life in her. "What are you doing?"

"I love your feet," he said huskily, holding her sock-clad foot in his large hands. "Have I ever told you that? So small. So delicate. I love—"

"Phil?"

"Hush, Victoria." He lifted his face to her, and she saw his eyes, dark with the same desire she felt. "I'm making love to you. Unplanned, unscheduled, with no stealth, no hiding. In a place that is uniquely ours." He raised his hands and rested them on her waist. A smile quirked his face. "Uniquely *yours*. A lovely, sylvan glade."

She felt her throat tightening with the flood of emotions washing through her. He had never mentioned their furtiveness before. It bothered her; she should have known it also bothered him. And she wanted this, the closeness, the rightness of their being together, wanted it so much she felt compelled to speak out against it. "This lovely sylvan glade," she said thickly, "is full of rocks, and four-legged, six-legged and no-legged critters."

"Hush, Victoria," he repeated softly, lifting her from the saddle and holding her against him. "For now, listen to your heart and not your head."

And she had done that, lying with him among the sweet-smelling grass, with sunlight dappling through the trees overhead, with no sounds but those of the stream and scattered bird calls and their own murmured words. She had once thought there was no sensitivity in Phil Wilcox. That afternoon he had proved her wrong, so very wrong, showing her sensitivity and gentleness and enough of the pagan to match their surroundings, and a desperation she had only sensed peripherally at the time.

Now that desperation haunted her. That had been the last time she had seen him. Had that been his way of saying goodbye? She pushed away from the window and stared unseeingly across the deserted classroom. No. If she knew anything at all about Phil, she knew that when the time came for them to part, he would tell her, not just fade from her life. But was that time imminent? Was he growing tired of her schedule, her problems, her needs? "Not yet," she whispered as she picked up her books and purse. "Please, not yet."

Phil wasn't at the ranch when she got home. She stifled her disappointment, telling herself it was no more than she expected. Pop came out from the shed where they housed the tractor, looking flushed and defiantly guilty as he wiped his grease-stained hands on a rag. "Wilcox called," he told her, not giving her time for her lecture about tearing into the workings of the recalcitrant brush hog without her there to help. "Said he wouldn't be able to make it out here this afternoon."

Victoria slammed the truck door, glanced at Pop, glared pointedly at the greasy rag he stuffed into his hip pocket, and started toward the house.

"He asked if you'd have a couple of hours for him this evening, after supper."

She stopped in her march to the house. A couple of hours wasn't time enough for a trip into Fort Smith, and it would be too damned dark to visit their "sylvan glade." Phil had to have talk on his mind, and he had never before scheduled time to talk, he had just taken it. Was this it, then? A formal, stiffly phrased goodbye?

"I told him you would," Pop said.

Pride kept her spine straight, her shoulders stiff, her eyes dry. She heard her father's steps behind her, then felt his hand drop onto her shoulder.

"You ashamed of seeing him, Vickie?"

"No!" Her denial echoed around them in the stillness of the yard, shocking her with its vehemence.

Zack studied her with the silent intensity that had had the power to send the child Victoria into a guilty squirm, whether or not she had any reason to be guilty. Although she had long since outgrown her physical reaction to his examination, her emotional one remained, fueled by his next softly spoken words. "Sometimes you act as if you are. I heard him ask you out to Sunday dinner week before last. I heard you put him off with an excuse about work."

She answered him calmly, levelly, betraying none of her emotions. "That wasn't an excuse. You know how much I have to do on Sundays."

Zack nodded. "Yep. And I know that work's something that's always going to be around. Is Wilcox?"

Victoria tensed even more under the softly spoken blows of his words.

"How long is a man like him going to be content with bits and pieces of a woman, Vickie? Seeing her a couple of hours here, a couple of hours there, when and if she decides to make time for him?"

Not long, she cried silently. *Maybe not past tonight.*

"You're going to have to decide if you want him, Victoria, and if you do, you're going to have to do something about it."

Want him? The need she felt for Phil went far beyond wanting. And there was nothing on earth she could do about it. Not now, for her—maybe not ever, for him. She twisted around to face the house. Pop didn't understand; she hoped he never would. Her father, and because of him, the ranch, were loving responsibilities she had willingly assumed, but she could never burden another person with them. Especially not Phil, who had once been married to a woman who saw him only as a means to money.

Pop's hand tightened comfortingly on her shoulder. "You're wearing yourself out. I want you to go in the house and rest for a while."

"You know I can't do that. The brush hog—"

"*I* fixed the hog."

She whirled to face him.

"And I don't want to hear a word from you about it," he said. "Not one. I'm not an invalid. I refuse to be one."

Because this was the first sign of spirit she had seen in him for weeks, Victoria's lecture died unspoken.

"Rest," he ordered her in a voice she had almost forgotten. "Then fix yourself up pretty. And when Wilcox gets here, you won't have a single excuse not to spend time with him unless you just don't want to."

THE SUN WAS a muted red glow, softening and silhouetting the mountains and casting long shadows across the highway as Phil drove north toward Victoria's place. Was he doing the right thing? Where Victoria was concerned, he didn't know. He pounded the steering wheel in frustration. Hell! Where *anyone* was concerned, he didn't know. And when had that happened?

Phil the fixer-upper. That was the role he had assumed at twelve when his dad died, first helping his mother with the two younger children, the housework, the never quite adequate income. Later he expanded the role to include his extended family, friends at college, neighbors, and clients in his law practice. *Got a problem. Take it to Phil. He'll know what to do.*

And usually he did. Sometimes without being asked. So why didn't he know now?

At least one problem seemed to be working out, he acknowledged as he thought back on his late-afternoon visit to his cousin David's ranch. Will. Without answers to the questions that still plagued him. Without the confrontation with Sam over what quite probably was an unfounded accusation.

In spite of a reasonable reluctance because of earlier trouble his children had had with Will, David had agreed to hire the boy and let him live on the ranch with his foreman. After all, David had said, if anyone could straighten out a troubled boy, crusty old Hank Baker was that person. Phil agreed. Hank had been surrogate father to David, to himself and his brother Ben. Will's arm was still in a cast, his ribs still in an elastic belt, but he did the work Hank assigned him, sometimes grudgingly, sometimes complaining that it was "kid's work." And he was still belligerent. But every once in a while, Hank had said, a knowing twinkle in his faded blue eyes, he had to work at being difficult.

After their conference with Hank, Phil had walked with David up to the ranch house, the modernistic stone-and-glass monstrosity that had never quite seemed a home until Leslie's arrival. Phil had never envied his cousin's money, but sometimes he did envy David the happiness he shared with his wife.

They entered the house through the French doors into the breakfast room, and Leslie came out of her adjoining office, a warm smile of welcome for David, an exuberant hug for Phil. "It's about time you got back out here," she told him. "It's been way too long."

Phil bent down and kissed her loudly on her cheek, winking at David as he did so. "It's been less than a month."

"That's what I said. Too long." Laughing, she extricated herself from the hug. "There's a fresh pot of coffee and some cake. I suppose you're starving, as usual."

Phil thought about denying her gentle accusation but grinned instead. With Leslie, pretense was never necessary. Neither was pretension. The three of them raided the kitchen then settled companionably around the table in the breakfast room.

Yes, Phil thought, feeling the affection that flowed between David and Leslie, sometimes he did envy his cousin. Not his past; no one could envy that. But his present. His future with the woman who had brought laughter and love back into his life. Everyone adored Leslie. Looking at her now, it was almost impossible to believe that only a few short years ago, she had thought that no one, not even her new husband, loved her.

Leslie glanced up at him, catching him as he lifted a forkful of chocolate cake almost to his mouth. "How is Victoria?"

Seeing the perception in her eyes, Phil hesitated. *No pretense,* he reminded himself. He lowered the fork to the plate. "Busy," he told her. "Tired almost to the point of exhaustion. Prickly as a cactus. And unwilling to take any help from me but what physical labor I can sneak in while we're together."

"I thought so." She reached over and rested her hand on his. "Have you told her you're in love with her?"

"My God. Is it that obvious?"

She smiled and shook her head. "Only to someone who knows you. Only to someone—" She glanced at David, a question in her eyes, and he nodded silently. "Only to someone who had a lot of experience trying to hide emotions. Will you accept some advice from me, Phil?" She hesitated, then, taking his silence as consent, continued. "Tell her how you feel."

He shook his head, withdrawing his hand from hers. "I've tried. More than once. She doesn't want to hear it."

"Or she's afraid to hear it," Leslie suggested. "Have you considered that?" Her eyes clouded. "She reminds me a lot of me, the way I was before David. Trying to hold up and hold off the entire world. She can't, Phil. No more than I could." She reached again for a hand, this time David's, and clasped it tightly. "What's going to happen to her when she realizes that?"

Phil glared at the encroaching darkness on the tree-shadowed highway and switched on his headlights. *Nothing* was going to happen to Victoria because he was going to see that she never reached that point.

Tell her he loved her? He wanted to. He had tried. Most people would scoff at the idea of Phil Wilcox not being able to say exactly what he thought or felt about anything. But he was the one who had been with her that first night in Fort Smith; he was the one who had been with her this past weekend on the hillside; he was the one who knew how hard Victoria worked at keeping what they shared on a strictly physical level. He grimaced as an unwanted thought struck him, and he rubbed at his beard, which had reverted to its usual slightly shaggy state over the past few weeks. What if she wasn't working at it? What if all she really wanted from him was an affair, physical release from the almost unbearable pressures she had to be under?

How ironic his daughter's words to him that morning seemed in the light of that possibility. Angela's reactions to his seeing Victoria had varied from inviting a relationship between the two of them to challenging one, from encouraging the time he spent with her to warning him the night she had caught him coming in so late on the dangers of ruining Victoria's reputation. And now this latest, mumbled around orange juice and an English muffin at the breakfast table. "Are you ashamed of seeing her, Dad? You never take her anywhere around here."

How could he explain to his daughter that in this insular community, for his age group at least, being seen out with a person more than twice was tantamount to announcing you were on your way to the altar, or at least to bed? How could he explain to his daughter that if it were up to him, he'd end all speculation about his and Victoria's route and have his ring on her finger? He couldn't. And he couldn't explain to her that Victoria, not he, was the reason they were not seen together.

Was an affair all she wanted from him? It didn't matter for now, he told himself. "The hell it doesn't," he growled into the silence of the car. He glanced at the lengthening shadows, then stepped on the accelerator. He wouldn't kill himself or anyone else, but he'd be damned if he'd let something like the threat of a speeding ticket keep him from her any longer than necessary.

When Phil arrived at the Tankersley ranch, he found Victoria asleep, curled up in a corner of the couch, her feet tucked under a hand-stitched quilt, her head resting on a small pillow and the soft light from a nearby lamp accenting the shadows beneath her eyes.

He watched her silently for a moment, knowing that no matter how much he had wanted from their evening together, he couldn't disturb her. Resisting the urge to pull the quilt up to cover her shoulder, to tuck a stray lock of hair behind her ear, to erase the small frown that marred her smooth, pale forehead with his fingers or lips, Phil turned quietly and reentered the brightly lighted kitchen.

He looked at Zack, ensconced at the table with the newspaper, rubbed at his beard and shook his head. "I won't wake her up."

"Better you than me," Zack told him, carefully folding the paper and placing it beside a stack of ranching magazines. "She won't appreciate either one of us letting her sleep." He looked up at Phil. "*You* she might not tear into, seeing as you just got here. I'm already in trouble with her." He pushed his chair back from the table and stood, leaning heavily on his cane. "I'm going back out to the shed. I left some tools out."

"Zack?"

"You going to lecture me about taking it easy, too, son?"

"No. No, that wasn't what I was going to say at all," Phil told him, letting his half-formed question about Zack's accepting behavior of him remain unspoken.

"Good." Zack glanced around the kitchen. "Damned little coffee. No tobacco. No whiskey. No wild women." He glanced back at Phil, and for a moment Phil thought he saw a twinkle of male camaraderie in the older man's eyes before it faded and Phil realized once again that more than one person in this household carried a heavy burden. "A man's got to have something. And for now... For now I guess I'm going to have to settle for the little dab of work I manage to get done." Zack paused on his way out the door. "Wake her up. She's expecting to spend time with you tonight. Got dressed for it before she fell asleep."

PHIL HESITATED at the edge of the couch, then knelt down beside her. Student papers lay scattered on the floor, as though they had slid from her lap, but an open book lay facedown, held against her by the loose clasp of her hands. Phil lifted the book from her. The ornate cover and densely printed text confirmed that it was an old book; the woman author and florid prose confirmed something else. He marked her place with a student paper and put the book on the coffee table before moving to sit beside her on the couch. "Victoria, Victoria," he whispered, "no matter how much you deny it, your need for romance keeps creeping back into your life, doesn't it?"

He felt an ache in the back of his throat. He wanted her to turn to him, not to some book. But how could he expect that, when she didn't even acknowledge her need? She would, he vowed. Some day. And when she did, he'd be there for her. And until then—he felt himself smiling—he'd just have to continue to settle for the little dab he managed to sneak in. He felt his smile slipping. Was he doing the right thing? He lifted his hand to her cheek. Of course he was.

He bent forward, placing his lips on hers. He felt her soft moan and the slight movement of her lips beneath his and increased the pressure of the kiss. Not taking, but giving. Giving her the love she refused to let him speak of—and that she was giving to him. Her lips parted, her hands raised to his chest. He kept his eyes open, watching hers, and knew the moment she came fully awake. She murmured his name against his mouth and slid her arms around him. Only then did he let himself get lost in the kiss, drawing her up to hold her tightly against his chest, silently communicating his love and his need for her, until he felt her drawing away. Reluctantly he released her mouth and loosened his hold on her.

She looked at him, then around the room, her confusion evident in her eyes. "I—"

"Shh," he told her. "I often wondered what would happen if you let yourself be still for longer than five minutes."

She rubbed at her cheek, ran her fingers through her wayward hair and laughed shakily. "Well, now you know. I'm sorry. I—"

She seemed determined to apologize for snatching much-needed rest, and Phil was equally determined that she wouldn't. Leaning forward, he silenced her the only effective way he knew—with his lips. He felt a flare of fierce response from her before she once again drew away. "Pop."

"Zack is being extraordinarily discreet," Phil told her. "He's gone out to the shed." He saw the concern in her eyes, quickly masked, and reached an immediate decision. He didn't know that the man was working, but even if he was, as Zack said, a man's got to have something. "He seems to be under the mistaken impression that you're not in the best of moods when awakened." He pulled her closer and nuzzled at her throat. "I wonder where he got an idea like that?"

Victoria laughed softly, bending her head back to give him freer access to her throat. "The shed, huh?" She slid her hands up his arms, his shoulders, to the back of his head, where they burrowed in his hair.

"Yeah." God he loved this woman. Soft and yielding as she was now. Passionate and demanding as she had been in their too-few private times together. Prickly and competent as she too often was forced to be. He'd take her any way he could have her. He felt a wave of desire shake him. But not here. Not in her father's house, with the possibility of Zack walking in on them at any moment. He was doing the right thing, and Victoria would agree with him, would recognize his real reason for doing what he had done. If he ever got around to telling her.

He succumbed to the temptation of one more lingering kiss before pulling away from her. "Do you feel like going for a short ride with me?" he asked. "I have something I want to show you."

Chapter Ten

He wasn't saying goodbye. That much was clear to Victoria, although she was still groggy and a little disoriented from her unaccustomed and too-heavy nap. She recognized the direction they were traveling, toward the lake. Lake Maline was one of the smaller Corps of Engineers flood-control projects, which provided a wildlife refuge, fishing and controlled hunting areas for sportsmen, and supplied several small communities, including Hillsboro and Styx Switch, with water.

She and Phil had never explored the lake area together, but his sense of purpose as he drove told her this was no aimless drive. He followed a series of country roads, finally turning onto a steep, climbing drive, and braked to a stop in a clearing of trees in front of a dark building.

"Wait here," he said. "I'll get some lights."

She sat in the car, studying the building by the headlight beams as Phil walked to what she now saw to be a compact log house, aged but cared for, and a suspicion worked its dark tentacles into the back of her mind. *This* was what he wanted to show her? A cabin in the woods? *Why?*

She saw lights come on in the cabin, and then the yard was illuminated by a floodlamp. She pushed her suspicions away as Phil returned to the car, determined to let him explain his actions before she jumped to any conclusion. He switched off the headlights and helped her from the car, leading her across a soft carpet of pine needles to the far side of the house, up onto a screened-in porch and into the cabin.

There wasn't much to see, and yet it was too much. Part of the sleeping porch had been enclosed and converted into a cozy kitchen and an efficient bathroom. The main part of the cabin was a single room, log-walled, a stone fireplace dominating one end. It was furnished with a comfortable sofa, two large chairs, a few tables and the lamps that provided the soft light that had spilled from the windows. At the other end of the room, partially hidden by a folding screen, was an ornate, iron-framed bed, neatly made up and covered with a colorful quilt.

"I...I took it in on a fee," Phil told her, watching her, almost as though gauging her reaction.

Victoria nodded, looking away from him, toward the fireplace. "Nice fee."

"Not really." She heard a thread of frustration in his voice. "I got the mortgage, too." She heard his steps on the hardwood floor, the soft thud of the door closing. "There are only a few acres," he said in a voice reminiscent of a tour director who wasn't quite sure of his material. "But there's a year-round creek on one edge of the property, and we're bordered on two sides by Corps of Engineers land. You can see the lake from the porch, and there's access to it, but we're isolated enough to discourage casual snoopers."

We, he kept saying. Her suspicions struggled their way back. She walked to the couch and touched an afghan folded over the back of it, an afghan that bore an amazing resemblance to one she had once seen in Phil's house.

"I know how busy you're going to be in the next few months. Haying season is coming on. And the end of school."

She felt her throat tightening. A lovely little hideaway in the woods. Just for the two of them. A place where they could go when there wasn't time for a trip to Fort Smith.

"I've had it leased out for the past few years," Phil continued. "When the lease expired, I decided—I decided I wouldn't do that again." She heard his steps behind her, knew that he stopped within touching distance of her but did not touch her. "I wanted to have this place ready sooner. If it had been...if it had been, I would have brought you here Sunday." His voice softened. "I'm glad now that it wasn't."

Victoria took a deep breath, trying to calm herself. Sunday and their time by the stream had seemed to her a natural and unplanned moment, and she didn't want to think about it here, in this cabin. She hated herself for her reactions to his careful plans. After all, she had made the ground rules, she had set the schedule. But right now she felt as though she were trapped in a hill-country version of the novel *Back Street*. "I see."

"No, damn it! I don't think you do." He dropped his hand to her shoulder and spun her around. She looked up, shaken by the anger in his voice and his actions and met his stormy eyes. With both hands on her shoulders, he held her immobile but did not pull her to him. "Do you realize that until tonight, except for that one time months ago, we have never been inside together, in anything other than a kitchen, a public place or a rented hotel room? Until tonight, I've never sat with you on a couch and held you in my arms? We've never had any place where we could listen to music, or watch a fire? We've never had any place where we could be alone to do anything we wanted, or nothing, if that's what we wanted. We need that kind of time together, Victoria. I need it. And so do you."

Her throat closed completely. She felt the press of unshed tears behind her eyes. She knew all those things he had shouted at her, knew them with a kind of quiet desperation, but she had convinced herself that Phil didn't mind. She lowered her head. With an oath, he eased his grasp on her shoulders and pulled her to him, holding her gently. She shook her head against his chest. *How long is he going to be content with bits and pieces of a woman?* Not long. And that was all she had ever been able to give him.

"I'm sorry, Phil. So sorry. It's a lovely place, and I—"

"No." He bent and kissed her cheek. "I'm sorry. I told you I felt clumsy and awkward around you. This just proves it. I shouldn't have blurted it out like this. I should have asked you. I shouldn't have yelled at you."

"Phil?" She twisted in his arms, reaching up to catch his face in her hands. "Will you please kiss me?" His left eyebrow raised slightly. "That's the only sure way I know for you to keep me quiet. Kiss me, Phil, before I say something else that doesn't need to be said." *Before I tell you how much I love you.*

PHIL DID NOT make love to her that night, almost as
though realizing that to do so would forever taint the
cabin for her. He did build a fire in the enormous
fireplace, slip a cassette into the player and open a
bottle of wine. Then he sat on the sofa, pulled her into
the crook of his arm and tugged the afghan down to
cover her feet. For a while he seemed like a man determined to enjoy himself, no matter how uncomfortable he was. For a while Victoria was equally
determined that he would enjoy the evening. He had
gone to a lot of effort to provide a place for them. For
her to deprive him of his surprise, any more than she
already had, would be cruel of her. Eventually, how-
ever, the firelight, the music, the wine and the warmth
of their closeness soothed her.

Phil felt the subtle release of tension in Victoria. He
sighed and turned his head, rubbing his cheek against
her forehead. His daughter's words that morning returned to haunt him. *"Are you ashamed of seeing her,
Dad?"* He wasn't; he thought Victoria knew that. But
her reaction to the cabin had been far from what he
expected; almost as though she, too, thought he was
hiding what they shared. And the truth was, they
didn't share enough; nothing short of a complete
commitment would ever be enough for him. He knew
she wasn't ready for that yet, but maybe she was ready
for more than they had.

Under other circumstances, Phil would have known
how to lead into what had to be said. With Victoria,
he didn't. With one palm gently caressing her shoulder, he looked over her head and fumbled for words.
"I—I want to take you places, Victoria," he said, answering the accusations he had felt from her even
though she hadn't spoken them. "It's selfish of me, I

know, but I want more time with you than we've had. I want to take you with me to activities in town; there aren't many, but some of them I have to attend, and I want you with me."

He felt the tension returning to her and steeled himself for the disappointment of her rejection. "The truth is," he said, speaking to keep her from doing so, then stopping, knowing that this was not the time for the truth. "The truth is, I want to be with you, anyway that I can, anytime that I can." This was a poor excuse for what he really wanted to say, but it was all, he sensed, that she would let herself accept from him.

You ashamed of seeing him, Vickie? Her father's words mocked her. No, she wasn't ashamed of seeing Phil. But she wasn't ready, yet, to make an announcement of their affair, wasn't ready to face the speculation that being seen together was sure to prompt. And she wasn't sure she would ever be ready to face the questions, well-meaning or otherwise, that would follow when Phil moved on, tired of the *bits and pieces* of her life that were all that she had to give him. She willed herself not to stiffen in his arms and murmured softly, "You know what my schedule is like."

"Yeah." The word came with a quick expulsion of breath. Phil had stilled his hand on her shoulder. Now he began a slow caress, sinking into silence for several minutes. Victoria shifted in his arms, needing his closeness, not knowing where this conversation was going and hoping he had abandoned it.

"And next fall?" he asked. "After you begin teaching full-time?"

Victoria closed her eyes. He hadn't abandoned it. So much for hope. But then, there wasn't much room for hope in her life. Not true, she thought. It was just that all of her hopes were concentrated on something else. Pop. If they were both careful, and if their luck held, Pop still had a good life ahead of him.

"Things will be a little better," she told him cautiously. "With my income, we'll be able to take care of some needed improvements, and to hire at least part-time help on a regular basis. But there won't be any miracle cure."

"There is a way," he ventured, equally cautious. "Interest rates aren't wonderful right now, but carefully invested, the money you'd get from selling the place and stock would give Zack a decent income."

She'd thought of that years before, thought of it and quickly abandoned the idea. She shook her head against Phil's chest and pulled away from him, not knowing how to explain but knowing this was something he had to understand.

"Have you ever heard my father's stories?" she asked, looking into eyes that were questioning, struggling to find solutions to an insoluble problem. He shook his head. She smiled, wanting to touch him but not doing so, struggling instead to explain something so nebulous it couldn't be real, but was. "There are dozens of them," she told him. "Going back for generations. About cowboys and Indians, lawmen and outlaws. It depends on which generation he's telling about, whether our ancestors wore the white hats or the black ones. But there's a common thread that runs through each one—the men and their land. And there are too many stories about the men of our family who abandoned the land only to die, sometimes tragically, always unfulfilled. So many stories, in fact, that it's become a truism among them." She shook her head again. "So, irrational though it might seem, moving my father to town, even if he would agree, would kill him as surely as putting him on a horse and letting him ride wild, the way he still wants to, across the hills."

Phil pulled her to him, not arguing, just holding her in a loose embrace with her head against his chest. She heard the beat of his heart, felt the long steadying breath he took.

"There's one thing wrong with your place."

She choked back a surprised laugh. There were lots of things wrong with her place, but she wondered what one thing a man who had an almost perfect setup of his own had singled out.

"It's large enough to work you to death," he said slowly, "and too small to make you any real money."

"I know."

"The—the Stevens's place next to you is for sale."

"I know." And she knew that as far as she was concerned, the land might as well not be on the market.

Phil's words came carefully, as though he was having to force each one. "That would give you the land you need for expansion."

"I know that, too." Now she chose her words carefully, praying Phil wouldn't take them personally. "But even if we could manage to come up with the down payment, Pop won't agree to another mortgage." She tried to pull away, but he held her more tightly and she felt a tremor in his arm.

"Of all people, I ought to understand that."

"No," she said quickly, insistently. "Don't even begin to think what I think you're thinking."

"I—I could help."

Now she did pull away. *He means well,* she told herself. *Remember that. He can't know how impossible what he's suggesting is.* Now she did touch him, lifting her hand to his cheek and seeing from the shadow of pain in his eyes that he did know. Slowly she shook her head.

"Why not, damn it?" His anger returned, leashed. "It would free you. It would free Zack. It would even—" he laughed bitterly and looked away from her, toward the fire "—it would even free me." He caught her face in his hands and looked deeply into her eyes. "Let me do this. I can afford it."

She forced her eyes to remain open, searching his, and fought the pressure she felt building in her throat. *Free him?* Free him from what? Was he harboring some guilt over what had happened years before? Or did he mean something else? Whatever he meant, she knew she could give only one answer. "I can't."

She watched his eyes close, felt the barely perceptible slump in his shoulders.

"Phil, look at me. Please." She had to tell him this, had to make him understand it. Now. "I can't take any more from you than I've already taken." There were others who would take anything this man offered, more than he offered. Even if she hadn't loved him, she could never use him, and she could never place herself in jeopardy of having him think she wanted no more from him than his ex-wife had. "I— I won't lie and say I'm not tempted by your offer. I even think I understand why you made it. But I won't take anything more from you than what you've already given."

He started to speak but she placed her fingers on his lips. "I can't take any more, because I can't *give* any more." Except honesty. She realized that she had never even given him that. She swallowed, still fighting the tightness in her throat. "You said something earlier about feeling selfish. You aren't selfish. You haven't done one selfish thing since we started seeing each other. I am . . . I have. But I—" She broke off, unable to meet his eyes, and hid her face against his throat. "I need to be with you," she said, her words muffled. "I want you so much."

A log in the fireplace crumbled, sending a shower of sparks before flaring, casting highlights over Victoria's dark hair. Phil held her loosely, afraid to try to tighten his hold on her with his arms or, now, in any other way. What had he expected? Not a declaration of love from her; that was too much to have hoped for at this time. But he'd hoped for more than the words of want, which, while keeping him in her life, kept him confined to a too-small corner of it—and kept him silent about what he needed from her.

"And I want you," he said, hoping that his voice didn't betray the degree of his need and the selfishness she had just told him he didn't feel. He didn't want to put any more pressure on her than she already had to bear.

VICTORIA STOOD by the door while Phil turned off the lamps in the room. He had banked and screened the fire, and she knew the low bed of coals would burn out safely before morning. She looked over the room, not smiling, but appreciating the beauty of it and the stamp of Phil's personality that was so evident. He was right. They needed a place that was theirs. She cringed inwardly when she thought of how much she needed him, of her admission to him of that need.

Thank God he hadn't picked up on it, hadn't pressed her for a deeper explanation of what she meant, because she was afraid that tonight, in this setting, she might have been weak enough to tell him.

He turned off the last light, locked the door and dropped an arm over her shoulder to lead her to the car. The moon had risen while they were in the cabin, lighting the rock-lined path. When he helped her into the car, Victoria smiled up at him. "I'm glad you decided not to lease it again."

Phil didn't return her smile, but he touched his fingers to her cheek before closing her door. When he eased into the driver's seat, he looked toward the cabin. The darkness and his beard obscured her vision, but Victoria thought she saw his jaw clench. It must have been her imagination visiting her unspoken emotions on him, because he turned to her, drawing her into a nondemanding embrace before starting the car and driving away.

GRAVEL SPAT from beneath the tires as Victoria spun her truck out of the parking lot at Johnson's Hardware.

"Damn!" she said, pounding the steering wheel with one fist and breaking the polite, strained silence that she had forced herself to maintain.

The load in the back of the truck shifted as she careened around a corner and reminded her again of the past several minutes. "Damn Eunice," she muttered, forcing herself to ease her foot on the accelerator but clenching the steering wheel. "Damn Phil." Because the signs of his meddling were all too clear. A front tire dropped into a pothole, shifting the supplies again, and Victoria pulled to the side of the road and stopped, knowing she had to calm herself before she killed herself or someone else. "And damn me, too," she whispered.

She shifted around to glance through the rear window at the supplies stacked in the back of the truck. Satisfied that they were secure enough, she faced forward and sat, shoulders stiff and arms stretched to grip the steering wheel. She shouldn't have taken them. If they hadn't already been loaded, she wouldn't have. In spite of the fact that she had two men scheduled to arrive later that morning to help with necessary repairs to the hay barn near the house. In spite of the fact that the nearest alternate source of supply was thirty miles away.

Well, she had taken the supplies. And she had paid for them. A profanity fell from her lips: one of her father's, used by him only when he had no idea she was within hearing distance. The words sounded alien in her voice and only moderately satisfying. The Tankersleys had had a thirty-day account at Johnson's for years, picking up what they needed through the month, settling up by the tenth. It was an arrangement that had been, for the most part, manageable, one that she had seen no need to change. Until today. Why was Phil doing this?

A city police car cruised by, the officer looking at her questioningly. Victoria shook her head and smiled at him. Then, her emotions as turbulent as when she had first pulled to the shoulder, she put the truck in gear and eased back into the lane of traffic.

The cabin. As they had too often in the past month, her thoughts centered on that isolated haven in the woods. She loved it; she hated it. Loved it, because at first with Phil, she could let herself pretend, let herself almost be the woman he seemed to want her to be. Hated it, because whatever it was that she and Phil had once shared had begun to change. Now, when they were at the cabin, there was too little time for talk, too little time for sharing, too little time for anything but their physical needs.

And now this.

She felt the tremor in her arms but couldn't release her grasp on the steering wheel. Was he working? She knew he sometimes went in on Saturday mornings but realized with a start that she didn't even know what his regular office hours were. So much for sharing, she thought bitterly. Had he never told her? Had she never shown him enough interest to ask?

She turned toward Hillsboro's small downtown area, found his office building, spotted his car at the curb nearby and parked her truck. What was she doing? She had no business barging in on him. She remembered the humiliation she had felt at Eunice's softly spoken words. The hell she didn't.

PHIL HEARD the discreet buzzer that signaled the opening of his outer door and suppressed a groan as Jack Jenkins, the elderly rancher seated across the desk from him, gathered up deeds and tax records and stuffed them into a worn folder. Jenkins, the uncle of one of Phil's ranch hands, was his third appointment of the morning, there were four more clients waiting in his reception area, and now someone else had come in. He'd never get out of here.

Jenkins shuffled to his feet and reached for his hat. "Appreciate you going over this for me, Phil. I feel a lot better about it now."

Phil smiled at the man and moved around his desk to open the office door. "Anytime, Jack. I just wish you hadn't worried about it so long before bringing it to me."

"If that know-it-all kid of mine hadn't kept after me with his damn-fool questions, I wouldn't have had to worry about it at all." Jenkins grimaced, but Phil knew that was the closest the man ever came to smiling. He accepted the man's hearty handclasp before looking up to check out the new arrival.

Victoria. In boots and work clothes. Phil felt a smile softening his face and the beginning of hope he had almost abandoned. She had never come to him before. Then he took in the confusion in her eyes, her colorless cheeks, and her stance, poised for flight near the door, and his smile faded. "What's wrong?" he asked her from across the room. "Is it Zack?"

"No. I—" Her glance skittered away from him, around the crowded waiting room, and returned to him. "You're busy," she said. "It will keep." Her lips tightened in a thin line as she spun on her heel and pushed out through the doorway.

For a stunned second Phil stood still. What will keep? Whatever was important enough to bring her here had to be too important for that terse denial. She was near the breaking point, he knew. She had been for weeks. Brittle and defensive except for brief moments with him and in spite of all his frustrated efforts to ease the load she carried. Something had happened, something important enough, or devastating enough, to bring her to him, and whatever *it* was, he knew it wouldn't keep. Without a word to his watching clients, he went after her.

She was already at her truck by the time he reached the sidewalk. He called out to her, but she didn't stop. Swearing, he sprinted after her, catching her by her arm through the open window just before she pulled out of the parking space. He spoke up, over the rumbling sound of the truck engine, but kept his voice as calm as possible. "What's wrong?"

She turned to look at him. The confusion was gone from her eyes now; they glittered. And her chin jutted at a determined angle. He felt the tremor that ran through her arm and eased his grasp. "What's wrong?"

She faced away from him, toward the row of store fronts, took a deep breath and squared her shoulders. "I told you I wouldn't take anything more from you," she said softly. "That goes for your family, too." She spun her head to look at him. "Call them off, Phil. We don't need any special favors, and we damned sure don't need any charity."

For the first time, he noticed the load of supplies in the back of the truck: sheet metal roofing, barn poles and a stack of lumber, and he began to suspect what must have happened. "Eunice," he said softly.

"You got it."

"What happened?"

She shook her head. "That won't work. You know what happened. Just see that it doesn't happen again."

She cast a quick glance over her shoulder, revved the engine and backed out into the street. Phil stood there, his denial unspoken, and resentment for all the other things he had had to leave unsaid growing, forcing out the worry he had felt for her.

VICTORIA WAS in the back of the truck, wedged between a stack of lumber and a stack of sheet metal, wrestling one end of a barn pole loose while Tink Harker lifted the other end. She saw Phil's car crest their hill and braced herself for a confrontation but handed her end of the pole over the side of the truck to Tink's brother and bent to lift another one.

Phil braked to a stop beside the truck and jumped out. "What in the *hell* do you think you're doing?"

Victoria sighed at his roared words, but she eased the pole back down and turned to face him. He marched around his car to the side of the truck nearest her, reached up, grasped her around the waist and swung her out of the truck.

He nodded at Zack standing nearby. "Your daughter and I are going to go have a talk. I'll bring her back. Later."

Zack pushed his hat back on his head and looked at them but didn't say anything. Victoria did. Digging in her heels when Phil took her arm and began tugging her toward his car, she did some yelling of her own. "I have a barn to fix!"

"And you have two strong men to do the work and a more than competent supervisor. Now, do you want them to fix the barn, or do you want them to referee what we're going to say?"

Chapter Eleven

Victoria felt waves of anger radiating from Phil across the distance of the car seat, but other than his first roared words, reminiscent of earlier times, he hadn't raised his voice. She remained quiet while they raced off the hill and onto the county road. She knew what caused his anger: *she* had, with her reaction that morning. She twisted around in the seat to stare out the side window at the countryside blurring by. Still, if she had been thinking instead of just feeling, she wouldn't have confronted him the way she had. She wouldn't have upset his office, subjected them to the speculation she had tried so hard to avoid, wouldn't be sitting here in strained silence knowing that her actions were inexcusable.

She recognized the direction they were traveling, toward the cabin. "No," she whispered.

He glanced over at her, his gray eyes the color of flint and about as soft. "Where else? Back to Zack and your barn builders? Or to my place with Angela as a witness?"

Sighing, she sank back against the seat. "All right," she said, swallowing her pride and daring to look at him. "I overreacted. For that, I'm sorry. But you know how I feel. And you ignored that."

Phil's jaw clenched; his hands tightened on the steering wheel. "I haven't ignored one thing about you for months."

"Phil—"

"Not now," he said tersely.

PHIL SLAMMED THE DOOR behind them when they entered the cabin. Victoria walked ahead of him, to the couch, watching the play of morning sunlight across furnishings and the special things that had made this room theirs for such a short time.

"Tell me," he said from behind her in a voice icy with control, "just what did my sister do that was so damned bad?"

"Don't pretend you don't know."

"Oh, I know now. I called Eunice after you left. At least you didn't open up on her with both barrels. I had to ask her for practically a word-for-word play-back of your conversation to find out what happened. And what do I learn? She offered you a revolving charge account—"

"We've never had one. We've never even asked for one."

"Victoria, my sister was left with four children to raise and a business that was one step ahead of bankruptcy. She's raised her kids by herself, and she's built a business anyone could be proud of. She knows pride. And she's not about to jeopardize her family or her business. Did you even consider that she might think you and Zack are valued customers? Or, based on your past account, a good credit risk?"

Victoria bit back an oath and took a deep breath. "And the discount?"

"She explained that to you, didn't she? Contractors get it all the time."

"But not ranchers, Phil. Not any that I know." Her fingers twisted in the afghan across the back of the couch before she turned and found him standing close to her, too close. "If you didn't ask her to do this, why me? And why now?" She heard the pain in her voice but could do nothing about it. "Because I'm sleeping with her brother?"

Phil swore a muttered oath as he closed his eyes and raised his face toward the ceiling. "No, damn it." He took her shoulders in his hands, looking at her but betraying no emotion in his eyes or his voice. "Because she knows that I'm in love with you."

His words hit her with the force of a physical blow. He loved her? He wasn't supposed to. If he loved her, too, it just made what they could never have more unbearable. "You—you told her that?"

"I didn't have to tell her. Anyone who cares about me enough to look has known for months how I feel about you."

Except her. Had she not cared enough to look? Or had she been afraid of what she might see? She lowered her face, hiding from his searching eyes. "I—" *Oh, God! What did she do now?* "I never meant for you to fall in love with me." She tried to twist away from him, but he wouldn't let her go.

"Never meant for it to happen—never wanted it to happen," he said with deadly calm. "That's something I'm just now beginning to understand." His hands tightened on her shoulders. "I've been told I'm perceptive. It's amazing how we begin to believe what we hear often enough. Being the perceptive person that I'm reputed to be, I thought I saw in your unguarded moments what I wanted to see, what I needed to see. And because of that, I stepped carefully around your pride, around your work, around your feelings. I don't hide things, Victoria, but with you and for you I have had to hide too many things in the past months. I felt like a married man, sneaking out for a forbidden tryst every time we were together. Sneaking around to see you. Hiding you from my family and friends. Because you wanted to be hidden. But I convinced myself that I could live this way because I do love you and that one day—'' he tightened his grasp on her shoulders, stopping just short of shaking her ''—one day you'd realize that you love me, too.''

"Phil—" She felt unwanted tears pooling in her eyes and futilely willed them not to fall. "I—I *can't* love you."

"I know." He released one hand on her shoulder, moving to her hair to fumble with the pins that held it in place.

"What are you doing?" she asked as her hair spilled over her shoulders.

"You once told me you were selfish," he said, lifting her hair, running his fingers through it. "I didn't believe you. After all the takers I had met, I found your reluctance to take anything from me refreshing. For a while." He moved his hand from her hair to the buttons of her shirt.

"Phil!"

"But you do take, Victoria, one thing at least. I just didn't accept until today that it was the only thing you wanted from me."

He lowered his mouth to her throat, to the shell of her ear, to the back of her neck, beneath her loosened shirt. She struggled to free herself from his hands, from his mouth, from the pain in his voice.

"Oh, no," he said softly. "This is the only thing you've ever let me give you, the only thing you've always taken from me. You do like this, don't you, Victoria—the pleasure I give you . . ."

She pushed against him, looking up at him through the blur of her tears and the cascade of her hair. She saw the pain in his eyes that matched the pain in her heart, before he captured her mouth with his in a kiss.

"What are we doing?" she asked on a shaky breath when he at last freed her mouth.

He twisted away from her, standing stiffly immobile, his head bowed. "It's called sex," he said slowly. "It's what you seem to think—it's *all* you seem to think we've shared."

Victoria lowered her face to her hands. She'd had little enough of herself to give, but had she given him nothing? How selfish was she? A moan broke from her, and Phil's head jerked up at the sound.

"No," she said, going to him and sliding her arms around his waist. "Oh, no," she told him again, shaking her head against his back. She felt his hands cover hers, holding her tightly for silent moments. Then he turned, taking her in his arms. She looked up at him, loving each line of his face, seeing the strain she had caused him. She wanted to tell him she loved him; her throat ached with the pressure of not telling him. But would telling him help, or only eventually hurt him more?

She lifted her hands to his face, running her fingers lightly through his beard before cupping his cheeks.

He looked down into her eyes, reading them, and she felt naked and raw, every emotion exposed, but she couldn't say the words she knew he waited to hear. His expression shuttered; his hands tightened on her back then released her, and Victoria stood there holding him, needing him, and knowing she had pushed him away.

"DA-AD!"

Phil looked up from his cooling coffee and the remains of his dinner as the exasperation in his daughter's voice penetrated his consciousness. "What is it?" he asked, realizing that his thoughts had taken him far from the comfort of his kitchen and the animated companionship of his daughter.

One side of Angela's mouth twisted up in a smile. "Welcome back. I was beginning to feel like I was talking to an empty chair."

Phil answered her smile with a rueful one of his own. "I think you may have been. What did I miss?"

"Not much," she admitted. "But I did ask you twice what you're going to do tonight."

Phil took a sip from his coffee, grimaced, pushed away from the table, and freshened his cup before answering with as much casualness as he could dredge up. "Not much. I thought I'd spend a quiet evening at home. Maybe catch up on some reading."

"On Friday night?" Angela asked incredulously. "Look, I know that Vickie's busy with the end of school and everything, and that you've been working really hard, but aren't you going to spend at least a little time with her tonight?"

Phil set his cup on the counter. This coffee wasn't any more tempting than the previous cup. "No."

Angela's eyes narrowed at his abrupt answer, then gleamed with speculation. "You've had a fight. That's why you've been walking around like a bear with a sore toe for the past week. You've had a fight with her and you didn't say one word about it to me."

A fight? What Victoria and he had been through was more like a major battle, a war lost, leaving nothing but desolation for both sides. He supposed that in the language of an eighteen-year-old, they had *had a fight*, but as far as saying anything to his daughter about how his hopes for the future had been ripped out of him.... "You know," he said, the loving understanding in his voice as hard-earned as his casualness had been a moment before, "I may have created a monster in you. Open communication is all well and good. I've encouraged it between me and you for too many years ever to want to remove it from our lives, but..." He picked up his coffee cup, studied its contents, then met his daughter's eyes, so much like his own. "Victoria and I have agreed not to see each other again."

"Why?"

He should have remembered the whys; he should have remembered that she was eternally curious and that he had always fostered her curiosity. He shook his head. "That's all you get. My right to share anything that's happening in my life stops when it infringes on another person's right to privacy. That's a lesson you should have learned from all my years in law practice."

"But Vickie's not a client," she said. "She's my friend."

"And I don't see any reason for that to change." He hoped it wouldn't. Victoria needed a friend. He doubted whether Angela could provide the kind of friendship that would truly help Victoria. Susan could, or better yet, Leslie, but he knew that the chances of Victoria accepting the overtures of any adult member of his family were almost—hell, not *almost*—*were* impossible.

"So," he said, signaling the end of the conversation. "A quiet evening at home—"

Angela dragged her head slowly from side to side. "Sorry," she said, sounding truly contrite. "Maxine and Jessica are coming out tonight to help plan our after-graduation party and to work on our prom dresses. They'll be here—" she glanced at her watch "—oh, Lord, any minute now. So I can't stop them." She grabbed the plates from the table and carried them to the sink. "I mean—you're always gone. This seemed like the best place to spread out our mess and not bother anybody."

"That's all right, Angela," he said, reconciling himself to the fact that the house would soon be filled with the sound of rock music and girlish laughter. He had always encouraged his daughter to bring her friends home; this wasn't some macabre act of fate designed to emphasize his sense of isolation.

She turned from the sink. "I can't stop them before they get here, but we could go somewhere else. Maxine's mother has a sewing machine. It'll take a little while to get gathered up, though. All the stuff is already here."

He shook his head. As much as he was not ready to be surrounded by youthful high spirits, he was even less ready to feel that he had driven his daughter from her home. "A bear with a sore toe, huh?"

She gave him a fleeting grin. "Yeah. But now that I know why, I kind of understand." She looked across the room at him, completely serious and much too adult for his comfort. "*You* ought to go somewhere, though. Instead of sticking your head in some old Bar Journal. When I broke up with Billy Jordan last year, you did everything but order me to go to Sandy's party. And you were right. I did have a good time. And my life wasn't over. And my friends were important to me. So even if you won't go out and whoop and holler—"

He had been right about something else. He *had* created a monster—a monster who remembered every bit of counseling he had struggled over and threw it back at him. "In Hillsboro?" he asked, interrupting her flow of words with an attempt at teasing.

She sighed, letting him know she wouldn't be side-tracked. "You could spend some time with Uncle Ben, or with David. You always used to like to do that."

He heard the blare of music through the open windows as a car pulled into the drive and the slamming of two doors and knew that he had to make a decision. He could lock himself in his room with a stack of journals and brood to the accompaniment of the latest rock group, he could chase his daughter out of her home and brood in silent isolation, or he could take some sort of positive action. Victoria was gone. She was no longer a factor in his life. That much, at least, was perfectly clear to him. Painfully clear. And understanding did nothing to eradicate the sense of loss, the frustration, or even the physical ache he still felt. But his life couldn't stop because of that.

He walked across the kitchen and dropped a kiss on Angela's cheek.

"What's that for?"

"All of a sudden I need a reason?" Her cocked eyebrow and continued silence told him that he did. "Let's just say it's for reaffirming what a good job I've done raising an exceptionally smart kid."

He expected a quick laugh from her, maybe a teasing comment. What he got was her quick flush, a grimace, and her words, muffled against his shoulder as she hugged him. "Maybe. Maybe I am. Sometimes I'm not so sure."

He had no time to question her. Maxine and Jessica opened the kitchen door and came in, laughing, carrying a grocery sack full of pop and chips, just as Angela pulled away from him.

He sat in his car at the end of the drive a few minutes later, trying to decide which way to turn on the county road. Telling himself he was going out to rejoin the human race and actually doing it, he had discovered, were two different things. Ben and Susan? Or David and Leslie? Both families would welcome a visit from him. He knew that without even having to question it. He sighed and slumped back in his seat. And both would remind him, just by their closeness, of what he would never have with Victoria.

Rejoin the human race? Not yet, he decided. Maybe he was acting like a bear with a sore toe as Angela had accused him. He knew only that for now, for a little while, healthy or not, he wanted to lock himself away in solitude to give his wounds time to heal. The cabin? For a moment he considered going there, lighting a fire in the fireplace although it was really too late in the season. But there would be no solitude there, not with his memories of Victoria's presence, of her coming to him by firelight, her glorious hair loose and cascading, covering them as she knelt over him. He glanced back at his house. The windows were open, and while he couldn't hear the sounds that passed for music, he could hear the underlying bass beat across the distance of the lawn. Phil rubbed at his beard, suddenly irritated by the mass of hair that hid his face. It had been a long time since he had had no place to go, no one that he wanted to be with. Swearing, he spun out of the driveway and turned toward town.

SOMETIME DURING the past semester, Wednesday had replaced Sunday as Victoria's least favorite day of the week. This one was no exception. She tried to tell herself that making the drive to the campus at Durant one night a week was infinitely preferable to making it three or four times a week, as she had in the past. She tried to tell herself that she only had a few more weeks of the commuting trip and not the years she had once faced. She tried to tell herself that at least one part of her responsibilities would be done with. It did no good. There was still the drive to make. Hours in the truck, going and coming, with her mind free to wander, as it had the previous week, to the one subject she knew it would do no good to explore. Phil. What she should have done. What she could have done.

She was late: late leaving her after-hours tutoring session, late getting away from an impromptu conference with her adviser at the high school, late finishing her chores, and, if she didn't hurry, she'd be late for her class.

She braked the pickup to an abrupt halt in her driveway and raced into the house. Zack was in the kitchen, stirring a pot on the stove. She mumbled a greeting as she hurried past him to the bathroom, where she gave herself a quick scrub to get rid of the aroma of barn lot, not recognizing that other, equally identifiable odor until she had a headful of shampoo lather. Pop's infamous camp fire stew. She groaned as she stuck her head under the faucet. Great. Just great. What was he going to do next?

His stew was wonderful, truly wonderful. He had served it to her when she was a child, along with stories of other times it had been served: around camp fires, on trail drives, during roundups. The fiery concoction also contained at least six items—maybe more depending on Pop's mood—that were in the restricted or just plain forbidden columns of his diet.

He didn't wait for her lecture. By the time she reached the kitchen, he had finished his supper, and she was secretly relieved. How many times had she had to caution him? She was beginning to feel more like his jailer than his daughter. And in spite of all her efforts, she was worried. He had aged years in weeks.

He had set a bowl of stew at her place, and Victoria approached it tentatively for that was the only sane way to approach his cooking. The chilies were obvious but not overpowering; the flavors of vegetables and beef combined in his own, unique blend. She sighed and attacked her first meal since breakfast in earnest.

"Knew you were running late," Zack said, leaning back in his chair.

Don't spoil it for him, she warned herself. Too few things in life gave him pleasure these days. If cooking for her did, then she would be properly appreciative. She'd worry about this breach in his nutrition later. She smiled. "Thanks."

He remained silent while she finished her meal, waiting, she suspected, for her to reprimand him about his diet and wondering why she didn't. She wondered why she didn't, too. Because she was tired? Because it never seemed to do any good? Because he never laughed anymore? The only things that seemed to raise him out of his depression were the letters he received from his brother Ted and never completely shared with her or the phone calls to New Mexico, which he hadn't mentioned but which had shown up on their last telephone bill.

The highly seasoned stew lost its flavor for her, and she pushed the bowl aside and reached for her coffee cup. She glanced across at her father and found him studying her with the same kind of intensity she had just devoted to him.

Oh, Pop, she thought, *what am I going to do with you?*

"Haven't seen Wilcox out here in quite a while. You two have a fight or something?"

Victoria closed her eyes briefly against the pain his words brought violently to life. She had fought for days against that pain, against her memories, only to have to confront it across the supper table. "Or something," she muttered grabbing dishes off the table and stacking them in the sink.

"That Saturday?"

Victoria clutched the edge of the sink. She started to ignore him, to pretend that she hadn't heard his question, but knew that would do no good. She nodded once, abruptly.

"What are you going to do about it?"

Do about it? There wasn't one thing she *could* do about it. "Nothing," she said. She wiped her hands on a towel. "Look, I've got to run or I'll be late to class—"

"Vickie, which one of you called it off? And why?"

She turned, and her slight weight sagged against the cabinet. She looked above her father's head for a moment, searching for calmness, before she met his eyes. "The why—the why is between us," she told him. She swallowed once, fighting tears that had threatened but had not fallen since Phil had brought her back to the house over a week before. "And it was a mutual decision."

HER THOUGHTS on her drive to class and home again were every bit as turbulent as she had been afraid they would be. Phil and her father. One, she had driven away from her, the other was slowly dying in front of her eyes, and she was powerless to do anything about either of them. She shouldn't have to choose between the two men she loved. She knew that both of them, if asked, would be quick to deny the need for choice. But the need was there; it was real. She couldn't abandon her father; she couldn't burden Phil with him.

The house was dark when she got home that night. She listened outside Zack's bedroom door until she heard his slightly raspy breathing coming regularly in the rhythm of sleep.

She'd made her choice, and it brought her no peace.

She was failing him. Somehow, someway, without knowing any other way, she was failing Zack as surely as she had failed Phil. *You can't do everything by yourself,* Phil had told her that last day. Could she? She had once thought so. *You once told me you were selfish. I didn't believe you.* He had said that, too.

And now he believed. Was she being selfish with her father? Was there someone, anyone, who could help him more than she could?

She stood in the dark hallway, her head resting in her hands, and felt the weight of every decision she had been forced to make weighing down on her. Then quickly, before she lost her nerve or talked herself out of it, she walked into the living room and picked up the telephone. There was an hour's time difference; maybe he would still be awake.

She counted the rings. On the fourth, a man answered in a gravelly, tobacco-roughened, younger version of her father's voice.

"Uncle Ted?" Her voice sounded small and hesitant, even to her. "This is Victoria."

"DA-AD?"

For once Phil didn't hear exasperation in his daughter's voice; he heard speculation—a speculation that prickled the back of his neck and caused him to look up warily. Angela stood in the doorway to his outer office. She had been busily pecking at his secretary's typewriter since they had locked the outer door to the building after his final Saturday morning appointment, and he had almost forgotten her presence as he at last got his brain in gear and settled down to research a pending case.

"Did you finish your term paper?" he asked, determined to ignore the alarm bells beginning to clang in the back of his mind.

She nodded, studying him with an intensity that raised the decibel level of the alarm bells. "Graduation is next week," she said slowly.

Now he nodded, waiting.

"I saw your picture in your college yearbook," she said. "You have a really nice jaw under all that hair." She cocked her head to one side, narrowing her eyes. "Maybe if you shaved."

I wondered about your beard. Phil heard Victoria's voice, felt again her first hesitant touch, smelled again the light floral perfume she wore that had never ceased to tempt and tantalize him. *I wondered how it would feel to touch it, to have it touching me.* He lifted his hand defensively to his jaw.

"Do you have a point to make," he asked his daughter, "or was that just an idle observation?"

"Observation." She abandoned her slouch against the door facing and straightened to her full height. "And—and maybe a point." She walked across the room and braced her hands on his desk, looking down at him. "We're running out of time."

He began shaking his head, knowing too well what point she had to make.

"I didn't think it was going to be this difficult," she said, "but now all we have is the summer. All right, I'll concede that there aren't all that many women around here who are suitable for you, and we really don't have time to start from scratch—"

"No," he said softly.

"But Maxine's Aunt Ingrid is in town this weekend," she continued, ignoring his interruption. "So maybe if you shaved your beard, you know, letting her see another side of you, and took her over to Fort Smith for a really super dinner—"

"No." This time there was no way she could ignore him.

Her eyes widened at the force in his word. "You liked her. You told me you did."

Phil closed his eyes briefly and took a calming breath. He'd thought Angela had abandoned her schemes, had thought there would be no need for this talk. How many other things would he be wrong about? "Angela," he said evenly, "Ingrid is a fine woman. I enjoyed the evening I spent with her last fall. But I have no intention of marrying her or any other woman just to fill up an empty house."

"Well, good grief, I hope not."

"What?"

"Nothing." She shook her head. "Look, Dad, you've got to help me with this. We agreed—"

"We agreed?" he asked incredulously.

"Well, kind of," she mumbled. "And it's Saturday, and I need to know what to tell Maxine."

Phil ran his hand over his face, praying for composure, before he rose and rounded the desk. "You set something up."

She took a step backward. "Not really, I just—"

He shook his head. "There's no telling what Maxine has said to her aunt, what Ingrid is expecting this evening. You can't play with people's emotions like that, Angela."

"I was just trying to do what's best for you."

He sighed. "Instead of making assumptions, why didn't you just ask me what I thought was best?"

"Well," she said, "what is?"

Victoria! Her name sprang to his lips, almost escaping before he captured it. And equally quickly, his own words mocked him. He had spent months trying to do what was best for the woman he loved, he'd made assumptions, he'd made demands, but never once had he said, "Victoria, I love you. What can I do for you? What can *we* do for *us*?" Was it too late?

He'd been harsh with her their last time together, unconscionably harsh, and if he were honest, he'd have to admit that only part of his actions had been a deliberate attempt to make her see that what they shared was not simply an affair but an expression of mutual, loving need. The rest of his actions had not been action at all, but reaction to frustration, to anger, to months of keeping silent.

He reached in his pocket for his office keys and tossed them at Angela. "Lock up when you leave," he told her, turning toward the door.

"Da-ad? Where are you going?"

"To do what's best for me." He paused at the office door and turned to his daughter, surprising a calculating smile on her face, which she quickly masked. "And you, young lady," he said, trying to keep his voice stern when all he wanted to do was hug Angela for finally showing him what he should have understood months before, "if you know what's best for you, you had better get busy and straighten out this mess you've created for tonight."

Chapter Twelve

Victoria stepped out onto the back porch, eased the screen door closed behind her, and lifted her face to the warm May sunshine. She arched her back, stretching against the tightness that sitting at the kitchen table for hours at a time never failed to cause, and smiled. Her own schoolwork was finished. Her students' term papers were graded. Now all that remained were final exams and graduation.

She inhaled deeply, breathing in the perfume of the honeysuckle that spilled in profusion over a portion of the garden fence. She was tired, but she wasn't exhausted. For the first time in years, she was able to understand what kind of pressure she had been under, simply by its absence. For the first time in years, she saw an end to at least some of that pressure.

Pop and his brother Ted came out of the tractor shed, talking animatedly. She heard the rumble of Zack's laughter mingled with her uncle's. Thank God, she thought. Calling Ted had been the right thing to do, had been the only thing to do. He'd arrived the second day after her telephone call, driving up in a rental car he'd gotten at the airport in Tulsa and brushing aside her worry that they were taking time he didn't have to spare, with the insistence that although he never had a free moment, he only had one brother. He had steadfastly refused to say anything about the letters and telephone calls, except "That's up to Zack to tell you, honey," but since Ted's arrival, she had seen Pop's attitude change, and his health seemed to improve as quickly as she had once seen it fail. And since Ted's appearance, she had glimpsed what life might be like on the ranch once she had income from her teaching position to support a hired helper.

The two men looked up, seeing her, and Ted waved his arm in salute. "We're going to the store to pick up some stuff I forgot," he called across the yard. "Do you need us to bring you anything?"

"No," she called back. "Have a good time." Her smile widened. The good time, she suspected and hoped, would include a cold beer for Ted at a tavern down the road where Pop had once gone, even after having to give up alcohol, to swap stories and to hold court. When had Pop stopped going? Sometime in the past few months, but like so many things that had happened or stopped happening, she had been too busy, too preoccupied, to notice its passing.

She stood on the porch until Ted's rental car disappeared down the hill and then wandered across the yard. Ted had stacked a couple of mineral blocks in the back of the pickup to take up to number two pasture. There was no hurry, she knew that, but she also knew with a strange sense of wonder that there was nothing else at that moment that she had to do, and God, how good that felt.

Josh and Jimbo saw her hesitating at the truck and came out from under the shade of the shed, tails wagging. She grinned down at the dogs. "Want to go, do you?'' she asked, and Jimbo gave an enthusiastic bark. ''Me, too,'' she said, laughing. The exercise would be good for her, and, for once, she would have time to enjoy the view of the mountains to the east. She patted the lowered tailgate of the truck, and the dogs jumped up.

Josh, the more affectionate of the two dogs, walked to the edge of the tailgate, nuzzling at her shoulder. She scooted onto the tailgate, dropped an arm over him and rubbed her cheek on his thick coat. Such simple pleasures. How long had it been since she'd enjoyed them? A sob caught in her throat, surprising her. ''Oh, Phil,'' she whispered, ''why couldn't you have waited?''

She tightened her hold on the dog, and he squirmed, licking at her hand. That wasn't the question, had never been the question. But what would have happened if he had not confronted her—if she had not forced the confrontation—until now? Now, when she could see at least a glimmer of hope.

There would have been no confrontation, she knew that. She would not have overreacted to Eunice's offer. She still cringed when she thought of her unreasonable behavior that day. She would not have stormed into Phil's office, would not have flung accusations at him, would not have run away from him, forcing him to come after her. The dog squirmed in her arms, and she released him. ''Spilled milk, Josh,'' she murmured as she jumped down and slammed the tailgate shut.

Or was it? She stood for a moment leaning against the truck. If she were to call Phil... Sighing, she shook her head. Things were a whole lot better, but they were a long way from wonderful. She would talk to Phil, she had to do that, as soon as she could find the words to explain that she hadn't meant to use him, hadn't meant to hurt him. But there was no way she could invite him back into her life, not for his sake, not even for hers.

She heard an engine groaning up the steep grade of the drive and straightened. Were Pop and Ted returning for some reason? If so, they didn't need to catch her mired in depression. But as she listened, she realized that the vehicle approaching sounded more powerful than Ted's rental. She swiped at her hair, smoothing it, tucked her shirt more tightly into the waist of her jeans, and turned, just in time to see Phil's car crest the hill.

PHIL HAD NEVER FELT less sure of his reception at the Tankersley ranch, not even months before in the first few puzzling times he had found himself drawn there. But he had to come. That much he was sure of. And he hadn't run here in blind reaction, either. That much he was sure of, too. He had reined himself in sharply after leaving his office and forced himself to take time to think, forced himself to examine his reasons for seeing Victoria again. He loved her; he knew that that one irrefutable fact colored his thinking. But he knew, aside from that, in spite of that, because of that, he needed to see her again. To apologize, if for no other reason. He'd hurt her. With all his good intentions, he had let his temper take over.

He crested the hill of the Tankersley drive and saw Victoria standing by the pickup, her slender figure a paradox of strength and vulnerability which never failed to tug at his heartstrings and call forth his protective instincts. His carefully rehearsed excuses for

being there deserted him, and he knew the one reason
why he had come. He had to be with her—today, tomorrow, the rest of their lives—and he, no, *they* had
to find some way to make that possible.

VICTORIA SILENCED the dogs with a quick command
and stood beside the truck while Phil parked his car
and walked toward her. Outwardly, she was quiet. Inwardly—her heart pounded a violent drumbeat
against her chest, and her thoughts flew chaotically. It
was almost as though she had summoned him up.
Another chance. Another chance, her heart cried.
Then she noticed his hesitation, the firm set of his jaw
discernible even beneath the lushness of his beard, and
the determination in his eyes, and she brought herself
back to reality with a silent, desperate thud. There was
unfinished business between the two of them. She had
just admitted that much to herself. Evidently Phil had
found his words of apology much faster than she had.

He stopped at the other end of the tailgate, leaving
the width of the truck separating them, and looked
down at the dogs who were waiting expectantly.

"Were you going somewhere?"

She heard resignation in his voice. How many times
had she heard that and not recognized it? "Just up to
number two pasture for a minute." *What is it, Phil?
This time, what do you want to do?* She almost said
the words. For the first time they were true. And for
the first time in a long time, maybe ever, she was more
concerned with his needs than her own. But while that
conflicting thought collided with her concept of what
had happened between them, the moment passed.

"Would you—" His lips lifted in the beginning of a smile then straightened and thinned. "Would you mind some company?" he asked abruptly.

"No. Of course not."

They remained silent while Victoria drove to the pasture, a silence broken only twice, when Phil got out of the truck to open and then reclose gates after she drove through them. And for Victoria, the quiet was underscored by other words, said and unsaid, and an endless replay of their last time together at the cabin, and the strained silence that had filled the car as he drove her home that day. He watched her intently enough, when he didn't think she was aware of it. Why didn't he speak?

The cattle, seeing in the truck a familiar source of food, fell in behind them when they reached number two and followed them to the small, covered feeder that housed mineral and salt blocks, but when no hay or grain appeared, went back to grazing nearby.

Victoria escaped from the confinement of the truck cab, dropped the tailgate and spoke softly to the dogs, giving them their freedom. It appeared as though if anything were going to be said at all, she would have to be the first to speak. So why was she finding it so hard to form words? She reached for one of the mineral blocks just as she felt Phil walk up beside her.

"Phil, I—"

"Victoria—"

They spoke in unison, in voices as strained as their silence had been, and she looked up at him, unable to hide her pain or loneliness or the love she had never admitted to him. He drew in a deep breath, expanding his chest, but then, instead of reaching for her as she thought for a moment he would, he turned and lifted one of the mineral blocks from the truck. "Just these two?"

She dropped her head, hiding the naked emotions in her eyes from him and hoping he would think her action nothing more than a curt nod as she lifted the other block. "Yeah."

The job took all of thirty seconds. Phil straightened from lowering the block into place and turned to study the herd. "They're looking good."

Victoria straightened and walked to where he stood, stuffing her hands into her hip pockets to keep from clenching them, or, worse, reaching for Phil. What was this? Surely he knew they couldn't just ignore what had happened between them. Surely he knew they couldn't go back—to what? They had never, *never* spoken this impersonally. "Yeah. They've... they've grown some. At least we won't be laughed out of the sale barn for bringing in a crop of runts." She glanced about for the bull calf of the yellow cow that showed just how little gain the rest of the calves had made, but when she didn't immediately spot him, she gave up the search. She had no reason to be concerned. The herd was closely grouped and grazing, with even some of the youngest calves nibbling.

The ground near the feeder was worn by trampling hooves. She kicked at a stubborn patch of grass that had somehow managed to survive, and it came up by the roots in a small shower of dust.

"You need rain."

"Mmm. But if it's all the same, I'd just as soon it held off for a week or two. We don't really have time to get in the hay right now. After graduation...." Her voice trailed off as she looked at him. He was no longer studying the cattle; he gazed toward the hazy blue outline of the mountains to the east, toward the view she had promised herself that she would enjoy this trip. He stood rigidly erect and had stuffed his hands into his hip pockets.

"How is Zack?"

"He's fine. His brother's here. He's been here a little over a week. Pop's fine. He's—"

"What I did was inexcusable."

Victoria felt her heart give a frantic lurch. Her throat tightened. "No." Her voice escaped with an exhaled breath, and she knew that the time for impersonal small talk was over. "No. Considering my irrational actions, I think you were—more than provoked."

He stood with his head thrown back, still facing the mountains, silent for a moment. "My daughter accused me of acting like a bear with a sore toe."

She forced herself to breathe. "Pop demanded to know what I was going to do about...about us."

"What are we going to do, Victoria?"

She closed her eyes and felt his hands, callused yet tender, gentle in their strength, framing her face. She looked up, seeing the questions and confusion that clouded his eyes. "There has to be some way we can be together without hurting each other."

"Without hurting *you*," she whispered.

He shook his head slowly, never moving his eyes from hers, and she saw in them what she had once tried to deny in his words. "Without hurting either of us," he said with quiet insistence.

He loved her. Victoria didn't know how or why, but at that moment she didn't care for reasons. He loved her, and she loved him, and without meaning to, she had shredded their emotions, leaving them raw and bloody in something that was never meant to be a battlefield. A moan escaped her as she stepped closer to him, sliding her arms around him. She heard his answering sigh as he lowered his arms to her back and pulled her closer still.

Phil held her comfortingly, passionlessly for several moments before lowering his head and finding her lips with a kiss that whispered promises, pledged forever. She answered him with unspoken promises of her own, stretching up to fit herself more closely against him, holding him, until slowly, reluctantly he broke the kiss and raised his head, still holding her tightly. "We have to talk."

She nodded. Yes. They had to do that. *She* had to do that, had somehow to find the honesty she had denied him, had somehow to find the words to attempt to heal the hurt she had caused him.

He dropped an arm over her shoulder and led her to the grove of trees where he had once kept vigil with her over an aging cow and a newborn calf. There, he settled against the trunk of an oak tree and pulled her protectively into the curve of his arm, sitting quietly for so long that a woodpecker in a nearby tree grew accustomed to them and resumed his search for food.

"Victoria—"

She raised her fingers to his lips, silencing him, fighting desperately to ignore how the touch of his lips on her flesh, even in this most innocent of gestures, affected her. "Let me. Please."

She felt the tension building in him, but he remained silent. Taking that for assent, she looked away from him, through the trees. "I never meant to use you," she said slowly, groping for words. "I never—

not once did I manage to convince myself that all we had was sex. I did—I did convince myself that, ultimately, that was all we ever *could* have. And because of that, I even—I even talked myself into believing that was all—that was all *you* wanted.''

Victoria felt his hand tighten on her arm. ''That's why, when you told me you loved me, I was stunned. I had this carefully constructed fantasy in which we met each other's needs for a while, a long time I hoped, and when you left—'' She drew a ragged breath. ''You weren't supposed to hurt, Phil. If I had thought— If I had dreamed there was a chance of hurting you, I would have called this off long ago.''

''And you, Victoria,'' he asked. ''Weren't you going to get hurt?''

She pulled away from him and rubbed her hands over her arms against the sudden chill. ''That was a foregone conclusion.''

''Why?''

He was asking for more than she could admit to him, even now. ''Because... because I had nothing to offer you.... Nothing but responsibilities and bills.''

He swore softly, and she felt his hands drop onto her shoulders, but he didn't attempt to pull her back against him. ''And the pleasure I found in just being with you? The pride I felt for you? You're so competent in so many areas, it almost scares me. You're so courageous, it shames me. And you're so hauntingly beautiful that just thinking of you robs me of the ability to think coherently about anything else.''

Victoria felt moisture in her eyes. She wasn't beautiful, not the way he meant, she was sunburned and windburned and scratched and nicked and callused, but with Phil—with Phil she had felt beautiful. She closed her eyes and lowered her head. "I'm not brave," she said. "And God knows, I'm not strong."

He moved closer, crossing his arms over her and drawing her against his chest, bending his head to rest his cheek against hers. "Maybe once you weren't. But you've taken what life's thrown at you, you've faced it, and you've gone on. That's courage, lady, that's strength, and I don't want to take any of that from you. I just want to be there for you, with you, to face whatever else is coming. And I want you there, with me."

Oh, and she wanted him with her, too. She was so tired of facing everything alone. But that wasn't the only reason or even the major reason she wanted Phil. She wanted his tenderness, his compassion, his understanding; she wanted to be the woman she felt herself to be when she was with him. Could she? Could they?

She twisted in his arms to meet his eyes. "There are so many problems. The ranch. Pop's health."

He met her probing gaze levelly. "I'm concerned for your father, but except for his health, which is in God's hands, not ours, is there really anything else that the two of us, together, can't find a solution for?"

She lowered her head to his chest with a long shuddering breath. Was there? At that moment, nothing seemed impossible. "This afternoon, just before you got here," she said slowly, "I was wondering what would have happened if we had waited until today to have our confrontation."

"And?" he prompted gently, warming her with slow strokes of his hands on her arms.

"The ranch is in the black," she said, feeling herself being drawn into the web Phil wove around her, a web that was so much more than physical. "There'll be a tiny profit, considering the poor showing of our calf crop, but if the market holds, there will be a profit. And Pop is so much better—I can't believe the improvement he's made in the past week. I'll get my degree in a few more days. And since Uncle Ted has been here, I've been able to see how much more freedom I'll have next year when we're able to hire full-time help.

"And I've missed you." She lifted her head, needing to see his face, needing to reassure herself that he was there, with her, and not a figment of frustrated dreams and longings. "I've missed you more than I thought it humanly possible for one person to miss another."

She felt the heat from his eyes boring into her, examining, waiting. "I want to love you, Phil," she said, forcing the words past the tightness in her throat. "I want that so much."

His eyes darkened and closed. He pulled her against him, burrowing his head at her throat and holding her tightly. She felt the erratic beat of his heart, the tension in his arms that became a faint tremor, his raggedly indrawn breath. "Thank God," he murmured. "I was afraid—I thought I had driven you away."

She felt tears running unchecked down her cheeks and for once did not fight them. "And I was afraid—" she choked back a tremulous laugh "—I was sure I had driven you away."

"Never, Victoria. Never. Hell itself couldn't keep me away from you." Then he was raining kisses on her face, erasing her tears, until, with a triumphant groan he found her mouth with his and pulled her down into the grass, covering her, shielding her, strengthening her with the love she felt flowing from him. And she shared her strength with him, matching him caress for caress, longing for longing, hunger for hunger. Their surroundings fell away—the woodpecker, the cattle, the distant shadowed mountains—leaving only the two of them. Together. One.

VICTORIA'S LILTING LAUGHTER surrounded them as Phil knelt beside her awkwardly tugging her boot back onto her foot. Still caught in the aftermath of a closeness none of their previous times together had even begun to prepare her for, she reached out and brushed aside the unbuttoned shirt he had so recently tugged on, to touch his chest with wondering fingers. "I once suspected you were a pagan," she said, her voice still husky. "Now, I have the proof."

He caught her hand with his and held it against him. "And you," he said. "You are a woods sprite, sent to tempt me and to raise me from the ranks of mortal men."

Contented laughter bubbled from her as she leaned back on her elbows, raising her face to the sky. "We did find paradise, didn't we?"

He leaned forward, as though unable to deny the appeal of her exposed throat. "Did we?" he murmured against smooth flesh and a pulse that quickened at his touch. "Or did we simply, finally, let it happen?"

"Does it matter?" she asked, reaching for him, loving the solid strength of his big body.

He shook his head against her throat, lowering her to the ground. "Nothing matters except—except—" She felt his body tense. "Victoria, I know this isn't romantic but—"

"But what, Phil?"

He groaned and rolled away from her. "There's something crawling up my back."

She lay there, fighting her laughter but finally surrendering to it. "You know we're going to pay for this, don't you? Once in the woods was tempting fate. But twice with no insect repellent?" She pulled herself up to a sitting position and lifted his shirt. Then, with competent fingers, she disposed of the brown tick determinedly marching up Phil's spine.

"What was it?"

"What do you think?"

He groaned again.

She studied his back and resisted the temptation to run her fingers over the smooth expanse of flesh. "If it will make you feel any better, I don't see any more, but I think we've been given fair warning."

Phil shrugged to his feet and held his hand out to tug her to hers. "As far as interruptions go, telephone calls are a lot more civilized."

Victoria grinned, loving the new lightness between them. "City boy."

He hugged her to him, giving her a mock threat with his fist for the insult, and joining in her laughter as they made quick work of finishing dressing. Arm in arm, they walked from the grove of trees toward the truck. The mountains loomed in the distance, the hillside behind the pasture marched upward in progressive shades of green, sunlight spilled its warmth from a cloudless blue sky. Victoria stopped, leaning against Phil, and drank in the perfection of the day, of the moment, before pulling reluctantly away.

"I'm almost afraid to go back," she admitted.

Phil hugged her shoulder. "We're together now, Victoria. That's something that's not going to change no matter what happens."

She smiled, holding onto the peace, the promise, his words gave her. "I'd better call up the dogs," she said. She reached in through the open window of the truck and gave one short blast of the horn. After a moment, when neither dog appeared, she frowned slightly and gave another, longer blast of the horn. Finally Josh appeared, without Jimbo, loping toward them from over a small rise, but when he reached them, he didn't jump into the truck bed. He whimpered once, barked sharply and circled, tail down, before turning and running a few steps toward the direction from which he had just come. He stopped, looked at them, and barked again.

"Something's wrong," Victoria said.

Phil nodded, sprinting around to the passenger door. "We'd better take the truck."

She knew there was no need to answer him. "Go boy," she said to the dog as she scrambled into the truck and started the engine. "Show us."

Josh took off at a run, with them bumping along behind him, past a thicket of wild dewberries in riotous bloom, around a rocky gully now running with a thin trickle of water, up another rise to a solitary locust tree near the northern boundary fence. There Jimbo stood guard over a single calf. Victoria recognized it immediately—the bull calf of the yellow horned cow that had given her nothing but trouble since she first saw it. The calf didn't even look at them as she braked the pickup to a stop. Instead, it looked wildly to its right, then plunged to the left in a headlong flight with the dogs after it, attempting to turn it before it ran into the fence. The calf veered again and came to an abrupt halt, head raised, eyes rolling, trembling.

"Oh, great," Victoria muttered. "Just what I need. A crazy calf from a crazy cow."

"I don't think so."

She turned to Phil, shaken by the seriousness in his voice. "What—"

"Look," he said.

She looked back at the calf. It lowered then lifted its head once, twice, as though attempting to butt at something, then sank to its knees and on down to the ground. Victoria glanced around, making sure the calf's mother was nowhere close, then jumped from the truck and ran to the downed calf, falling on her knees beside it. "What is it?" she asked Phil who had reached the calf at the same time as she.

Holding the calf's head down, he lifted his hand from its forequarter and turned to her. "Feel," he said.

She stretched out her hand. The calf's hide was hot and taut, too tightly stretched, and as she moved her fingers over it, she felt bubbles beneath the hide breaking under her touch. She jerked back her hand. "Oh, God." She couldn't move. *"Oh, God!"* For long seconds she knelt there, paralyzed, with her hand outstretched. Then, with a vengeance, feeling returned, and her strength fled. She sank onto her heels.

PHIL SNATCHED UP the telephone the moment they returned to the house, getting through immediately to his cousin David. She tried to leave; the horses had to be saddled, the stock trailer hooked to the pickup to bring down the one downed calf, but he grabbed her hand, holding her by his side.

"About a hundred and seventy-five calves in four pastures with two sets of working pens," he said tersely, relaying the necessary information. "Yes. There are good, level spots in both of those pastures. No. Just enough vaccine for the calves; the adult herd has already been vaccinated. Right. Thanks."

He hung up the telephone and looked at her. "Quit beating yourself for this," he said. "You took the same gamble most of your neighbors have taken, one that I've taken in the past, and you and I both know that could be the only infected calf up there."

Cradling the receiver beneath his ear, he dialed another number, still holding onto her hand.

"Who now?" she asked.

"My foreman. We'll need more horses and more men."

THEY WERE CROSSING the kitchen, headed toward the barn, finally giving vent to Victoria's need for physical action, when the kitchen door opened and Zack and Ted walked in. Pop's face split in a wide smile, and he stuck out his hand. "Wilcox. Good to see you again." Then, noticing their tension, his smile faded. "What's wrong?"

There was no good way to tell him. Victoria spoke as dispassionately as possible. "We have a calf down in number two pasture. It looks like blackleg."

Pop blanched. For a moment he seemed even more stooped. Then he straightened his shoulders and lifted his head. "Then what in the hell are we doing standing around in the kitchen?" He turned to his brother. "Didn't think you were going to get a chance to be a real cowboy while you were here, did you?" He turned to leave the room. "Come on," he said. "Let's get those calves rounded up."

"Pop!"

"Zack?" Phil's calm voice overrode hers.

Zack turned toward Phil, narrowing his eyes.

"David Nichols is on his way out here with vaccine and two sets of portable working pens," Phil told him. "My men will probably get here before he does. Someone is going to have to point them in the right direction. I don't feel comfortable enough with your operation to be the one to do that."

Zack agreed, reluctantly, to be the one to stay behind. Ted and Victoria left on horseback to round up the cattle in number two. Phil took the truck to trailer back the downed calf. When he returned with the calf, his men had arrived and had been dispersed by Zack. Phil surrendered the truck and calf to Zack, mounted his horse and rode to join Ted and Victoria. When the three of them brought the first of the herds into the corrals, David and his crew had just arrived. Zack accepted an armload of supplies from David and began pointing out gates and pastures. Then he turned, marching with determination toward the first set of pens and calling out orders to a couple of waiting hands.

"Pop!" Victoria cried, flinging herself off her horse and running to him. "What do you think you're doing?"

"I'm working my cows, Vickie, like a man's supposed to."

A trickle of blood ran down her cheek from a greenbriar scratch, her hair had worked its way loose from its pins, and her face was streaked with dust. She reached for him, grabbing his arm. "Pop, you can't do this," she pleaded. "You know what the doctors said. Your life is at stake."

Zack sighed and patted her hand on his arm. "Vickie, honey, when are you going to learn that ranching *is* my life? Now, there ain't nobody up in number three pasture. Would you rather I did this, or go up there and bring those calves in?"

VICTORIA WENT with Phil to number three pasture. With the dogs and two men she vaguely recognized, they found and brought the herd in to the set of corrals nearest the house. She stood in her stirrups trying to see what she knew was impossible to see, the other set of corrals, her father, how he was holding up. A towheaded boy waited at the pens for them with a supply of syringes and vaccine. Phil dismounted and walked to her side. "Together, Victoria. Don't forget that," he said. Then, ignoring the men and the noise and the milling, bawling cattle, he lifted her from her saddle and held her close. "He'll be all right," he promised.

Then there was only noise and dirt, the bellowing of the cattle, the clang of metal as the squeeze chute opened or closed. Separate the calves from the cows, run them through the alley, trap them, vaccinate them, isolate the symptomatic ones; over and over and over.

She looked up once, during a lull, across the sea of trailers and trucks that littered the yard and saw two unfamiliar cars arrive. She recognized Susan and Leslie. The women of the family closing ranks, she wondered, come to give aid and comfort? Sorry, ladies, she thought, dodging a kick and slapping another calf on the flank to send it through the alley, but I don't have time to play the role. When she saw the grocery sacks they lifted from their cars she immediately regretted her ungracious thoughts, but after that there was little time for thought.

Dusk threatened. She glanced up again to see rings of headlights in the distance illuminating the portable working pens, before the headlights where she and Phil worked came on, illuminating the scene around her with surrealistic intensity and blinding her to anything else.

Chapter Thirteen

It was over. Unbelievably. One by one the sets of headlights surrounding them were switched off, until Victoria was left standing in the dark, exhaustion clawing at her. Phil walked to her side and draped his arm around her, guiding her toward the house. He stopped beside the towheaded boy who had met them, hours before, it seemed.

"Good job, Mike," he said softly, and Victoria heard exhaustion in his voice, too. "Looks like David's going to make a cowhand out of you yet."

The boy grinned. "That's what he and Hank keep telling me."

The women had placed basins and soap and towels at the outside faucet, long tables piled with sandwiches and pitchers of tea and coffee along the front of the house and two washtubs of iced-down cans of beer near the steps to the back porch. Phil guided her to the faucet, where they scrubbed most of the grime from their faces and arms, then to a lawn chair, which had appeared from somewhere, and gently pushed her into it. A moment later he returned, handing her a napkin-wrapped sandwich and a mug of steaming coffee. "You need to eat something."

"Pop?"

"Leslie said he's gone down to talk to David. He's fine."

Victoria nodded. "I'll be back in a minute," Phil told her. "Eat."

Victoria sat in numbed silence, listening to the voices around her. Number two pasture was finished, number three, number one. That left only number four. She heard Phil's voice in the background. "Where's your shadow, Hank?" And a deeper, gravelly voice she didn't recognize, answered, "You mean the Hastings boy? He's working the dead wagon. He said that because of his cast that's all he'd be able to handle without getting in the way."

The voices drifted into a nebulous murmur. She closed her eyes and twisted her head, trying to ease the tension in her neck. She felt the coffee mug lifted from her hand and opened her eyes to see Leslie standing beside her. "I think you need this more than you do the coffee," Leslie said, handing her a can of ice-cold beer.

"You're right," Victoria admitted. "Thanks. And thank you for—" she gestured toward the tables. "Thank you for everything."

Leslie smiled at her. "That's what friends are for, Victoria. Although that's something I had to learn the hard way."

With a cryptic smile, Leslie left her. Victoria stretched in the chair. The last ring of lights was dark now. The men from number four pasture would be coming in soon. That meant Pop would be coming back to the house. By some miracle, he was all right; Phil wouldn't lie about that. Something else would be coming to the house with the men of number four. The final tally.

She heard the sounds of pressure-induced familiarity around her: the pop of beer cans being opened, the snick of a cigarette lighter, the laughter of comrades and the beginning of the war stories that would spread and grow. "Did you see that cow try to climb the fence?" one man asked another. "I sure thought old Harry was going to be singing soprano from that fool stunt."

She'd hear the tally soon enough. Right now, she couldn't face it. Right now, she wouldn't be missed. She eased from the chair and wandered into the darkness.

PHIL FOUND HER in the barn much, much later. She'd dragged a bale of hay over to the doorway and sat on it, leaning against the doorjamb, nursing her now warm beer, and looking toward the south, toward a gulley she couldn't see because of the distance but toward which she had watched the lights of a tractor make its way three times already.

Blackleg. Everybody worried about it, but nobody *worried* about it. Vaccinate your cows; vaccinate your keepers. Why waste time, energy and money on calves that are going to market? How long since there had been an outbreak in this area? She couldn't remember. She lifted the can for another swallow and found it empty. Pop had run cattle on this spread for at least twenty years without an incident. A spore, a tiny little spore that lived in the roots of grass and could lie dormant for— *God!* how long? And a vaccine that was so safe it could be bought over the counter and so effective it virtually guaranteed protection if the animal hadn't already ingested the spore. "Don't work them unless you have to," Pop always said. "No point in stressing them any more than necessary." She couldn't blame Pop; she'd gone along with him. But, damn it! she should have argued this point. She wasn't a gambler. She crumpled the beer can as she saw the tractor lights making their way back to the gully.

Death, like birth, was no stranger to the rancher. Every place around had their equivalent of the gully. A boneyard. A place where the occasional carcass was dragged. Usually, although she knew the people she had once thought her friends back east would never understand, the carcass was just left there for the coyotes and other predators to pick clean. Usually there wasn't so much death. There would be fires tonight.

She felt a large hand drop comfortingly onto her neck and looked up to see Phil standing beside her. "Thank you for today," she said quietly. He scooted onto the bale beside her, pulling her into the curve of his arm. Today, for the first time, she hadn't resented his help; for the first time, she had accepted it as he offered it, in love; for the first time, she had seen how things might have been between them. And his family—his family had been wonderful.

She took a deep breath and squared her shoulders. "Do you have a final count?"

His arm tightened. "Seven so far."

She flinched; no matter how much she thought she had been prepared, she wasn't; not for that number.

"Five from number two pasture, two from number three. It looks like one and four were clean. Two more are symptomatic. It doesn't look good."

"Nine."

She felt the brush of his beard across her forehead as he shook his head. "One calf was trampled in a chute and had to be destroyed. One cow, an old one, just keeled over. Zack says from stress and age. David agrees with him."

"A red one?" she asked, and wondered why her voice sounded so calm. "From number two?"

"Yeah."

"She has a new calf. Was it one of the ones—"

"No."

Eleven. Maybe twelve if none of the other cows would take the orphan. She couldn't cry. For the first time in her life she wanted the release of tears. Her eyes burned, but they were dry.

"It's bad, Victoria, but it's over."

"It's *bad*? Oh, no. It's a lot worse than bad, and it's a long way from over. And it's so...so *damned* unnecessary."

She found herself rocking back and forth on the bale. Phil caught her in his arms and stilled her. A red glare came from the direction of the gulley, and another.

"Do you know what that is?" she asked him in a monotone.

"Yeah."

"I don't think you do. That's not just a funeral pyre. That is hell, Phil, and in spite of what you said earlier, it will keep us apart."

He twisted her around, holding her by her shoulders. "What are you talking about?"

"You know as well as I do what this means."

"Do I? This is a setback, Victoria, not the end of anything. A few hours ago we were talking forever.

Together. Not a roll in the bushes. Not for-better-but-get-the-hell-out-when-things-get-tough.''

"Sorry." She pulled away from him and stood up, taking a step backward. "I just changed the rules."

"Why?"

"A few hours ago you convinced me I had something to give you. Now I know just exactly what that is. A crazy, wonderful old man who insists on working himself into another heart attack or stroke. A ranch that would be in bankruptcy court tomorrow if we had a mortgage payment to make and might be, anyway. A thousand acres of hill country land that need enough improvements to beggar a much richer man than you. And a motley assortment of livestock that you wouldn't even allow on your own place."

"And you?"

"Oh, yeah. Me. I'm the worst deal of all, Phil. I'm empty. Absolutely empty. There's nothing of me left."

GIVE HER TIME, Phil had told himself when she turned and walked away from him that night. But as the days passed, he wasn't sure that had been the right thing to do. He wasn't sure that time was what Victoria needed. And he wasn't sure how long he would be able to stay away from her. He saw her at Angela's graduation, but she either didn't see, or pretended not to see him. The night of Victoria's graduation ceremonies arrived, and he saw his daughter off to Durant, still arguing with himself that staying away from Victoria was the best thing he could do for her.

TED STAYED for her graduation, driving Victoria and her father the one hundred plus miles to the college campus in his rental car. His visit had continued to be good for Zack. In spite of the strain of the roundup and subsequent cleanup operations, Zack looked better than he had in months. He stood taller than he had in a long time, only leaning occasionally on his cane, and in his Western-cut suit, a virtual duplicate of Ted's, he looked handsomer and younger than she could ever remember.

They separated at the football field, and Victoria hurried below the stadium to don her robe and cap and line up for the procession. She had attended one graduation ceremony at Vassar. This was far different. The college band provided the music as the graduates marched across the football field to folding chairs set up for them before a banner-draped platform. The loudspeaker squawked feedback until a harried technician loped onto the platform and adjusted the microphone. The speeches droned on while Victoria waited, alphabetically near the end of the line, for a moment that should have come ten years before.

No, she thought, looking around her at other adult graduates and at fresh-faced, optimistic young people, this was a long way from Vassar. A soft breeze made its way across the field, riffling the tassel on her cap. And her future was a long way from the one she had once envisioned. No Ivy League college waited with baited breath to offer her a teaching contract. The closest things to Sheraton or Hepplewhite furniture she would ever have were the faded and comfortable remnants of her mother's youth. And the eager students who would wait for pearls of wisdom to drop from her mouth, more often than not would have mud on their jeans and a mouthful of either tobacco or profanity. And Brad—she surprised herself by thinking of Brad at that moment; he hadn't crossed her mind in months. She didn't miss him. She rolled his name around her mind trying to summon up some emotion and found none, not even bitterness.

The president of the college was announcing names now, slowly, allowing time for the smattering of applause that greeted each graduate who walked across the platform. He was only up to the *D*s. Victoria settled herself for the wait. After ten years, a few more minutes would pass like—would pass like hours. Because she knew what she missed. A moment of weakness, of reminiscing, had breached her defenses. Phil. She clenched her hands tightly together in her lap and willed her mental walls back into place. She had made her decision; the pain would go away. Maybe in a thousand years. Maybe. Her row stood up. She stood with them, moving with quiet precision, her heels digging into the turf of the field until she reached the protective matting leading to the platform.

"Charles Talmadge," the president intoned and waited for the smattering of applause. "Maxine Tamplin." Victoria climbed the steps of the platform and waited while Maxine marched across. "Victoria Tankersley."

She bent her head and the dean of students shifted the tassel from one side of her cap to the other. No applause. But she shouldn't have expected any from Pop and Ted. She marched to the center of the platform. A loud and exuberant cheer went up from the bleachers. Stunned, she turned and spotted a banner with the words "Way to go, Vickie!" emblazoned on it in red paint. She recognized Angela's bright red hair before she recognized the girl. And Lydia Benton and Jimmie Foresman. Two more of her tutoring pairs.

The president of the college shifted slightly so that he couldn't be seen from the audience and grinned at her. "Looks like you've made some young friends," he said in a low voice as he shook her hand.

Victoria's eyes misted as she nodded, but no tears formed. She looked back at the crowd, Yes, she had made some friends. *Ivy League,* she thought, abandoning decorum and throwing her hand up in a signal of triumph toward her cheering section, *eat your heart out!*

AT HOME THAT NIGHT, Zack dragged a bottle of champagne out of the back of the refrigerator. He also brought out three glasses, but after wrestling the cork out of the bottle he only poured a taste for himself. "To you," he said, holding his glass out in salute. "To you," Uncle Ted echoed in his cigarette-roughened voice. "To me." She giggled when the first bubbles hit her nose, whirled around in a quick dance step and sank onto the couch, allowing herself a moment of triumph.

The dogs had come in and settled themselves on the cool stone of the hearth. The room was pleasant, she admitted. More than pleasant. She had her father with her. She had her Uncle Ted, who had proven to be a wellspring of strength for her and Pop. She had her career. And if it was humanly possible, they'd keep the ranch. She didn't have Phil. She pushed that thought away, as she had consistently pushed it away since that night at the barn; only each time, each time it was harder to do.

Pop cleared his throat and tugged his tie loose. "I have a present for you, Vickie."

She smiled. "That's not necessary. My whole education was your present to me."

He flushed. "You know that's not true. You earned it. Every bit of it." He reached for the album sitting on the coffee table and pulled out a long slender envelope, which he handed to her before returning to his chair near the fireplace.

Still smiling, she opened the envelope. There was a card. Where he'd found it, she'd never know. On the card was a caricature of an octogenarian cowboy seated on an equally aged, swaybacked horse. Both of them wore graduation robes and caps. Chuckling, she opened the card to read the message, and a folded paper fell into her lap. She picked it up, puzzled, opened it and skimmed the words, then she looked up, even more puzzled.

"You've earned that, too," Pop said, "and more."

"What is this?" she asked, knowing what the paper was, not knowing what it meant.

"It's the deed to this house," he told her, "and one hundred and sixty acres surrounding it, going all the way up the hill to that creek you like so well, all the way down to the road. There's enough land for a horse and to run a few cows if you really want to do that, but not so much that it will work you to death, ever again."

She shook her head slowly, looking from her father to her uncle. "I don't understand."

"You've got a new life for yourself now, Vickie, and I'm—I'm going home."

"This is home," she insisted.

He shook his head. "This is your home. This was your mama's home. It's never been mine. Not really. Those hills you love, they make me claustrophobic. I'd have gone back years ago, Vickie, right after your mama died, if I hadn't felt I'd cheated you out of one chance at school already."

"But what—what are you going to do?"

Zack looked toward his brother. "Ted and I have been talking about it for months. I was only waiting till I was sure you were through down there to say anything. Ted's got the same problem we did, Vickie, not enough cash and not enough people to do what needs to be done. The people who bought the Stevens's place to the north of us wanted this place, too. With the money I'm getting from the land, and what I'll get from my share of the stock, I'm buying back into the homestead."

She was across the room, kneeling at his knee, without knowing how she got there.

"What are you saying? You're going out there to work? Pop, what have the doctors told you time after time after time?"

"I'm a hell of a good cowboy, Victoria," he told her, and she knew that only the intensity of trying to make her understand allowed him to use language he thought too strong for a woman's ears. "There are things I can't do anymore...I know that. But there are things I can do, and still do better than most other folks. And one of those is telling other people how to do what I can't. You ought to know that."

He lifted his hand to her cheek and tilted her face toward him. "Vickie, honey, you once asked me what good it did to be able to see forever when there was nothing to look at. Let me ask you this. What good does it do to live forever, when there's no reason to live?"

Victoria dropped her head to her father's knee while his words sank into her, enveloped her, mocked her. He'd freed her. With a few words and a piece of paper and logic she couldn't refute. Now. Now that there was absolutely no reason to be free. Victoria laughed. Surprising her father. Surprising her uncle. Surprising herself. Her laughter echoed around the silent room, building to a crescendo before breaking off abruptly. Then, she cried.

Chapter Fourteen

Phil found a parking space on the perimeter of the crowded sale barn parking lot and walked around to the other side of the building, to the mobile home where the Hastings family lived. Just as David had suggested in his telephone call, Phil found a white pickup truck with the green Nichols logo parked in front of the trailer. Avoiding the makeshift steps, he reached up and knocked on the trailer door. There was no answer, but that didn't surprise him. Judging from the sounds coming from the barn and the number of people leaving, the sale had just broken up.

He returned to the sale barn and entered the building. Avoiding the crush of people at the cashiers' windows, he walked over to the concession stand. "Is Will around?" he asked. Mrs. Hastings, a washed-out, worked-down woman, turned from scrubbing the grill and grimaced. "He's out back with Sam, I think."

Phil nodded. He went outside, skirting the arena, and reentered the shed area of the building where penned cattle waited for their new owners.

They were out back, or so Mrs. Hastings thought. And if what he thought was true, they'd be way out back. Phil could no longer deny or rationalize his suspicions, especially since David had added to the growing list of "coincidences." With only brief nods to acknowledge greetings, Phil marched toward the distant, poorly lighted, less-crowded region of the shed.

He heard Sam's voice before he saw him, raised in anger yet muffled by the shouts and noises from other areas of the stock pens. "Lazy, good-for-nothing, smart-mouthed, know-it-all kid," and the distinctive sound of— Phil sprinted forward, rounding a corner too late to see the actual blow but in full view of the tableau lighted by one bare, hanging bulb. Will's arm, recently out of his cast, still shrunken and pale, was caught now in Sam's punishing grasp. Sam's face was a dull, mottled red; Will's, twisted in a grimace.

Phil took a step forward, but another man walked out of the shadows, not seeing Phil, focusing instead on Sam and Will. Zack Tankersley. Phil had only a moment to wonder what Zack was doing there. Zack's mouth tightened, baring his teeth, before stretching into a hearty grin that didn't fool Phil for a minute.

"Sam Hastings?" Zack called out. "That your voice I hear back there?" Sam loosened his grip on Will's arm just as Zack stepped into view. "And your boy?" Zack asked. "Of course it is." Casually, as though he had heard nothing, suspected nothing, Zack stepped between father and son. "Good boy you've got here, Sam." He thrust out his hand toward Will. "Never did get a chance to thank you for all the fine work you did for me the other night, son. You ever need a job or a recommendation, you look me up."

Will took Zack's outstretched hand, looking confused. "But—"

"I said, you look me up. You understand, boy?"

Will nodded, dropping Zack's hand and stuffing his own hands into his jeans pockets.

Phil took another step forward, feeling a reluctant grin forming. Victoria's father had talents Phil had never suspected. With a patently false smile, a few well-chosen words, and a tact that Phil could never hope to emulate, Zack had defused a potentially violent situation. But now it was Phil's turn. He couldn't avoid it any longer; he had put it off too long.

He took the few steps necessary to put himself in the circle of light, nodded at Sam, looked questioningly at Zack, and spoke to Will. "David sent me to look for you. He needs the supplies in the back of the truck."

"Wait a minute," Sam said. "I need him here."

Phil shook his head. "Sorry. The boy's on probation, you know that. And one of the conditions of his probation is a full-time job." He glanced at Will. Was that a flare of relief he saw in the boy's eyes, or resentment? "Tell your mother you're going to have to cut your visit short. Hank Baker needs you in the hay fields this weekend. I'll be out Monday afternoon with your probation officer to go over your work schedule."

With a quick nod, Will stepped around Zack and disappeared into the shadows, leaving Sam red-faced but silent.

"Good to see you, Wilcox," Zack said.

"Good to see you, too, Zack," Phil said. *For more than one reason.* "Are you going to be around awhile? I need to talk to you."

Zack nodded. "Thought you might." Then he, too, disappeared into the shadows, leaving Phil alone with Sam Hastings.

"So he's doing a lousy job for Nichols, too?" Sam asked as he bent and retrieved his fallen hat. "I swear, there ain't nothing going to straighten that boy out."

"On the contrary," Phil said carefully. "David has no complaints with Will's work or his attitude. In fact, seeing him at work out there is almost like looking at a different boy."

Sam pushed his hat back on his head and fixed narrowed eyes on Phil. "What are you saying?"

"Asking, Sam. I'm asking something I should have asked months ago and didn't, because I didn't want to believe there was any reason to ask. Is there something you need to tell me about your relationship with your son?"

"You mean like why I can't get him to do one damned thing I tell him to?"

"No. Like what you do to him when he doesn't do what you tell him to do."

Sam's face flushed even more, and his eyes bulged slightly. "Oh, hell, yes. I take a belt to him now and then. That's what you mean, isn't it? But you've got a teenager. You know what they're like. Don't tell me you never whipped your kid."

Not since she was five years old and had scared him senseless by trying to climb over the fence to pet a new calf that was penned with an overly protective mother. "I never broke her arm," Phil said. "I never cracked her ribs."

"And you think I did those things to Will?"

"I'm asking, Sam. Just asking. Like I'm asking about the split lip David tells me Will came home with the last time he stopped by here to see his mother, the one he swears he got when he didn't dodge a pothole and banged his mouth on the steering wheel. Like I'm asking about what I heard but didn't see while I was on my way down here to talk to you. Is he going to have another bruise today, Sam?''

Sam muttered a short, violent expletive. "You wouldn't believe me if I told you he swung that punch, would you?''

"Did he?''

Sam didn't answer; he just glared at Phil.

"What are you going to do?''

Best for me? Will's words mocked Phil. *You do that, Wilcox. Just as soon as you figure out what that is.* Where had he gone wrong? What had happened to his good intentions? When had he strayed from being Phil the fixer-upper to playing God, without the omnipotence of God? Never again, Phil swore. Never again would he impose his concept of what was right for someone else on another person.

Phil sighed. "What I should have done months ago. What I was told to do months ago but put off, out of a misguided sense of loyalty to you and to Will, thinking *I* could handle it. I'm going to take this to the juvenile authorities. I'm going to let people trained to do this job figure out what in the hell is going on.''

Sam took one blustering step forward. "I hired you to keep the boy out of jail, Wilcox, not for any other reason.''

"Wrong," Phil told him. "You hired me to represent your son, and it's time I did just that.''

PHIL FOUND ZACK two sets of pens away, with one booted foot resting on a bottom rail and his elbows resting on the top rail, staring out over a swarming herd of cattle. Phil rested his elbows on the rail beside Zack's. "Did you see who swung that punch?''

"Nope." Zack swiveled his head to look at Phil. "You going to do something about it?"

"Yeah."

Zack nodded and looked out over the cattle. Phil raised his booted foot to the bottom rail. "What are you doing out here today?"

"Selling out."

"What—" Phil jerked around to face the older man.

"And before you get all in a dander," Zack told him, "this is a want-to sale, not a have-to. Vickie's out of school. I've got nothing to keep me here now, and I'm going home."

"And Victoria?" Phil asked through a suddenly dry throat. "Is she going with you?"

"Nope. This is Vickie's home."

"How is she?"

"Hurting. And it ain't all because of me. But right now, she's busy convincing herself how tough she is." Zack snorted. "Remember that yellow cow, the one that gave her so much grief?"

"You mean the one that almost killed her."

"Yeah. That one. Well, for a day and a half after that cow lost her calf, couldn't no one get close to her. Meanest, most cantankerous, most worthless cow I ever had on the place, and I've had some rank ones. Vickie had been bottle-feeding the orphan calf because none of the other cows would even let it get close. I took that calf and put it in the pen with the yellow cow. The damned cow took it. Three snorts and a nudge, and that calf was nursing.

"We brought all our stock in for today's sale. It took us three days and a rented trailer to get them all down here. You know what Vickie did? She took one look at the buyers and figured out real quick that that pair was going to get separated, that nobody but a packer or canner would be fool enough to buy that yellow cow. She had me pull them out. That's how tough she is."

Phil lowered his head and rubbed at his beard.

"I like you, Wilcox. I always have. What are you going to do about my daughter?"

"Damned if I know, Zack," Phil said, at last voicing his own doubts. "I'm not sure there's anything I can do."

"Bull!" Zack turned around and leaned back against the railing. "You have got to be two of the stubbornnest people I have ever seen in my entire life, both of you! Stiff-necked, prideful and too damned *noble* for your own good. Do you love my daughter or don't you?"

"Hell yes, I love her. And I've tried every way I know to convince her of that."

"Have you?" Zack asked. "Have you now?"

"Yes. Every way. Up to and including pleading with her."

"Well, now, it seems to me that a tough girl like my Vickie wouldn't want a man to beg." He glanced up at Phil. "It seems to me you don't beg those witnesses in court, and you don't beg those juries. Remember how you got her to go out to dinner with you that first Sunday?"

"Yes, but you're not supposed to know about that."

"Ain't nothing wrong with my hearing, boy. And remember how you got her to go with you that Saturday you had the big fight?"

"Victoria doesn't need—"

"Vickie needs to admit what she needs. And if you're half as smart as I think you are, if you use that head of yours for anything other than hanging a hat on, you ought to be able to figure out how to get that to happen."

Could he? Nothing in his life had ever been more important. "Where is she?"

Zack grinned. "Out on the east side of the barn, loading that cow."

Phil shook his head. If he was going to convince her, and he wasn't completely sure he could, only that he had to try, he needed all the help he could get. He paused long enough to ask one favor of Zack. Zack's laughter rang through the shed before he caught Phil's hand in a hearty grasp and nodded his agreement.

THIS HAD TO BE the stupidest stunt she had ever pulled in her entire life. Victoria blew a stray lock of hair out of her eyes and tugged on the rope. She needed this cow like she needed a hole in her head. Another hole in her head. To match the one that had let her brains escape. She tightened her hold on the rope. Even with the calf already inside, the yellow cow was having nothing to do with the stock trailer. "Get in this trailer, damn it!" she muttered to the cow. "Or I swear I will leave you here and *let* them turn you into dog food."

"You pull," a deep voice called from behind Victoria. "I'll get her started."

Oh, God, she thought. *Phil.*

She heard Phil's yell and the swat of his hand against the cow's flank, and the cow plunged up into the trailer in a replay of that first time, months before. Victoria secured the rope and reluctantly turned to face him as he slammed the trailer gate shut.

He stood looking down at her, not smiling. "It seems to me we've done this before."

She nodded, not speaking.

"Some folks would take this as an omen," he continued, "meaning that—maybe we should start over."

She sighed and shook her head.

"You're right," he said stepping closer, and she had to tilt her head to see his face. "Starting over won't do for us at all, will it, Victoria?"

No, she thought, looking into his eyes and trying to read what she hoped he couldn't see in hers. Too much had happened for them ever to start over.

"I saw Zack inside. He told me he's leaving."

She pulled breath into her lungs and turned away from Phil. "Yeah." She straightened her shoulders and found her voice. "I thought what I was doing was for him. He thought what he was doing was for me. It seems that we were both wrong."

"Were you?" She felt the warmth of his body next to hers as his hand dropped onto her shoulder. "We could have all saved ourselves some pain if we had just talked with each other."

"But we didn't did we?"

"No. Not then." His hand tightened on her shoulder and he moved slightly so that they faced each other. "It isn't too late for us, Victoria."

"Isn't it?" She couldn't bear to look at him, but he filled her vision. She concentrated on his shirt pocket. When hadn't it been too late for them? Ten years ago? When she was still able to dream, plan, hope, feel some genuine unselfish emotion? Or had she been able to, even then? "I think it is. I think it's always been too late."

"Why are you doing this?" he asked, dropping his other hand to her shoulder and holding her prisoner. "You know you love me."

"Phil, please. I—I really have to leave."

"Not now," he said. She looked up and read only determination in his eyes. "Not this time. Not unless you leave with me."

Oh, no. Not with him. She'd convinced herself that what she was doing was the right thing, for him if not for her. But there was no way she could face him with her reasons, not without saying far more than she needed to say. Not now. Maybe not forever. "Sorry," she said. "I have other plans."

"They've just been cancelled."

Never again, Phil had just promised himself, and he meant it, but he knew that he had to make one exception. For both their sakes.

She met his steely gray gaze that was filled with a resolve she had never seen before with an icy determination of her own. "No."

"Yes. You and Zack didn't talk, and look what a mess that got all of us into. You and I are going to talk."

"No."

His hands shifted on her and before she could splutter a protest, he lifted her and slung her over his shoulder.

"What in the *hell* are you doing?"

"That's my line," he told her, ignoring her kicking, and carrying her across the parking lot. "And ladies don't swear. Isn't that what your father told you?"

She squirmed on his shoulder, looking up, but when all she could see were the men in the lot, laughing, nudging one another, pointing at her, she dropped her head and began pummeling Phil's back with her fists. "Put me down," she insisted. "You're making me the laughingstock of the county."

"Then quit fighting. You're making the scene, not me. You need to learn to be carried with dignity."

"Like a sack of feed," she muttered, but she quit struggling.

"Now," he said companionably, "to answer your first question, I'm staking my claim on you. It would have been much simpler if you had just agreed to go into town with me for dinner two Friday nights in a row, but I guess this method will get the word out almost as fast."

"You're crazy, you know that?"

"Unfortunately, I do."

When they reached Phil's truck, he carried her to the driver's side, opened the door and scooted her in, following quickly and fastening her seat belt around her. "Stay in the truck," he warned. "I'll just chase you down and carry you back."

Victoria cast a baleful glare at him, but she could still hear laughter coming from the parking lot. There was no way she was going to face more of that. "All right," she said. "You wanted to talk. Talk."

"Not here." He started the engine and pulled out of the parking lot, spitting gravel from beneath his tires.

Victoria shrank back in her seat. "Then where?" Why was he doing this? "The cabin?"

He turned to look at her then directed his attention to the road. "We'll go back there sometime. I have a lot of fond memories of that cabin. But not today.

We're through sneaking around. We're through hiding, from other people and from ourselves."

PHIL PULLED TO A STOP in the driveway beside his house and reached for her. "I can walk," Victoria told him.

"I know that. Unfortunately you have a tendency to walk away from me."

He lifted her, once again slinging her over his shoulder, and carried her into the house through the front door.

"Oh. Hi, Dad."

Victoria cringed at the surprise and curiosity in Angela's voice and shuddered when Phil turned so that his daughter could see who he carried over his shoulder.

"Hi...uh...Vickie."

"Angela," Phil said reasonably, "you are my daughter and I love you. You are the light of my life and the hope of my old age. But right now I want you to go down the hall, get your toothbrush and your nightgown and go spend the night with Maxine."

She heard Angela's giggle. Phil stood in the hallway, holding her, until the girl returned. Angela paused at the door on her way out of the house. "I...ah...goodbye, Vickie."

Victoria hid her face against Phil's back. "Goodbye, Angela," she muttered.

Phil carried her into the living room and dumped her on the sofa. Victoria leaned back against the comfortable cushions and hid her face in her hands. "I suppose you think you have some reason for humiliating me like this."

She felt the couch cushions shift as he sat beside her, and then his hands claimed hers, pulling them away from her face. "I would never intentionally hurt or humiliate you."

She tried to free her hands, but he refused to let her. "Then what was all—all *this* about?" she cried.

"I love you," he told her, "but for some reason I can't seem to get that one simple fact through your thick head. And you love me, but for some reason known only to you, you won't admit it. So *this* is where we get those two facts straight between us, our families, our friends and anyone else in this county who is curious enough to wonder just what we are to each other."

"We're nothing to each other."

"We're everything to each other. Past, present and future. And you love me."

"Phil, we had a—a time when I tried to be the woman you want."

"You *are* the woman I want. And you love me."

"I'm not! I'm hard and grasping and unfeeling."

"And loyal and dedicated and loving. And you love me."

"I'm single-minded, and career-oriented and self-ish."

"So much so that you spent an entire week helping a student who wasn't your responsibility try to reach a dream. And you love me."

"And I'm so perceptive I almost killed my father trying to do what I thought was best for him."

"Is that what you're doing, Victoria? What you think is best for me? Because you do love me."

"Phil, look at me! My calluses have calluses. It's been years since I've had fingernails worthy of putting polish on. I'm scratched and sunburned. Ninety percent of the time I'm in jeans encrusted with mud."

"You're a woods sprite who showed me the way to paradise, a wraith who came to me by firelight. And you do love me."

"There's not a romantic bone in my body."

"You read those nineteenth-century romances and try to convince yourself that's true. But it isn't. And you love me. You've argued everything else, but not that."

"I hurt you!"

"Yeah. Yeah, you did. And you hurt yourself, too. You want to hear your reasons? I think I can remember them. Maybe it's time to examine them. A crazy, wonderful old man. Well, Zack's taken charge of his own life. We can love him, but he refuses to let us be responsible for him. A ranch on its way to bankruptcy—taken care of. A thousand acres of hill country land that need extensive improvements—ditto. A motley assortment of cattle that I wouldn't allow on my place. Well, you don't have a single head that I wouldn't allow here. As a matter of fact, you don't have a single head. I bought that yellow cow and the calf from your father. They're being delivered tomorrow. And you love me."

He bought the cow? A cow that no one in his right mind would have on his place? He bought her?

"Say it, Victoria. Three words. Just once. Say it!"

"All right, damn it! I—"

Her words echoed around them in the room. She leaned forward, mouth open, not believing she had almost voiced them, but they reverberated in her ears.

Phil's head jerked up. He watched her carefully, one hand outstretched but not reaching for her. He drew his lower lip between strong white teeth then let out a careful breath. "It's not so hard, is it? Now once more. Finish it, Victoria. I—"

Victoria drew in a deep shuddering breath. She did, she really did love this man. Why couldn't she say it? "I—"

"Love—" Phil prompted.

The word hung in her throat. "I—"

"Come on, baby, just two more words. That's all."

"I—" Victoria looked into his eyes and tried to hide her growing panic. She *couldn't* say the words. Not even now that she wanted to. Ridiculous! She wanted to say them. Wanted to believe and *did* believe that Phil wanted to hear them. *I love you.* Simple words. Words people said every day.

"I—" With a moan she flung herself against Phil's chest. "I love you." Saying them once freed her voice. "I love you, Phil. I love you. Damn it! I love you."

Phil gathered her close in his arms. "I know," he told her gently. "And I love you."

She lifted her face from his shirt and looked into his eyes. "I know," she said. And with that knowledge came another knowledge. She was the woman he wanted. Whoever she was. *All* that she was. Her.

"Once more," he said again. "Without the profanity."

She saw laughter in his eyes and felt her own laughter bubbling up. "I think you're pushing your luck asking for so much so soon," she told him. "I think it's going to take a lifetime to get that worked out."

He pulled her tight against his chest and burrowed his face at her throat. "Victoria," he said, and his breath whispered warm promises against her flesh, "you have got yourself a deal."

There was no hope in that time and place
But there would be another lifetime . . .

The warrior died at her feet, his blood running out of the cave entrance and mingling with the waterfall. With his last breath he cursed the woman. Told her that her spirit would remain chained in the cave forever until a child was created and born there.

So goes the ancient legend of the Chained Lady and the curse that bound her throughout the ages—until destiny brought Diana Prentice and Colby Savagar together under the influence of forces beyond their understanding. Suddenly each was haunted by dreams that linked past and present, while their waking hours were fraught with danger. Only when Colby, Diana's modern-day warrior, learned to love could those dark forces be vanquished. Only then could Diana set the Chained Lady free. . . .

Next month, Harlequin Temptation and the intrepid Jayne Ann Krentz bring you Harlequin's first true sequel—

DREAMS, Parts 1 and 2

Look for this two-part epic tale, the

Temptation

"Editors' Choice."

Harlequin Temptation dares to be different!

Once in a while, we Temptation editors spot a romance that's truly innovative. To make sure *you* don't miss any one of these outstanding selections, we'll mark them for you.

EDITOR'S CHOICE

When the "Editors' Choice" fold-back appears on a Temptation cover, you'll know we've found that extra-special page-turner!

THE

Temptation

EDITORS

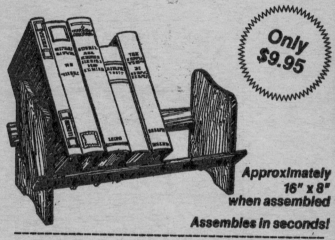